CARNAL
MACHINES

CARNAL MACHINES

STEAMPUNK EROTICA

EDITED BY
D. L. KING

CLEIS
PRESS

Published in the United States by Cleis Press, Inc., 2246 Sixth Street, Berkeley, California 94710.

Printed in the United States.
Cover design: Frank Wiedemann
Cover photograph: Hartmut Nörenberg
Text design: Frank Wiedemann
Cleis Press logo art: Juana Alicia
First Edition.
10 9 8 7 6 5 4 3 2 1

Trade paper ISBN: 978-1-57344-654-9
E-book ISBN: 978-1-57344-675-4

Contents

INTRODUCTION

The Victorians wrote some of the best and most enduring erotica. For such a tightly laced age, people spent a lot of time thinking about things carnal. And, speaking of tightly laced, I love the feeling of being laced into a tight corset; the constriction; the way the fabric encases my body and hugs my curves. It makes me feel powerful. But that's a tale best left for another time.

Writers such as Jules Verne, Sir Arthur Conan Doyle and H.G. Wells enthralled us with their visions of new possibilities during the steam age. They, of course, didn't use the term *steampunk*. That was our generation's answer to the pressures of the technological age (that's the age after the space age—there are lots of ages). We find it somehow comforting to go back to a simpler time but, because we can't do without our technological marvels, we recreate them as they might have been made in the steam age: steampunk.

But what was that about corsets? Oh, yes, corsets, tightly

laced carnality. Steampunk, even without sex, is erotic; with sex, it's over-the-top hot. Just think of all the deliciously erotic machines that could be run on steam power or a rudimentary form of electricity. The authors of this anthology thought of little else, or so it would seem.

A widowed lady engineer invents a small device that can store the energy from sexual frustration and convert it to electricity to help power a home. Teresa Noelle Roberts shows us what it can do, confronted with sexual fulfillment.

What volume of steampunk would be complete without a tale of sailing ships and the men who sail them? Poe Von Page introduces us to the mutinous crew of the *Danika Blue* and its new captain. Of course this ship sails the solar winds of space rather than the sea, and the captain has quite the interesting relationship with the ship's redheaded cartographer, with her delicate features, ecru eyes, black lace dress and charcoal-smudged fingers.

Then there's the very special room on the top floor in the *House of the Sable Locks*, a brothel where sexually discriminating men go to have their fantasies fulfilled. Even if a man daren't put those fantasies into words, Elizabeth Schechter's "Succubus" will give the madam all the information she needs to make her clients happy.

Within these tales are brothels, flying machines, steam-powered conveyances, manor houses and spiritualist societies. The following erotic adventures afford intelligently written, beautifully crafted glimpses into other worlds, where the Carnal Machines won't fail to seduce you, get you wet or make you hard—so lie back and relax; a happy ending is guaranteed.

D. L. King
New York City

HUMAN POWERED

Teresa Noelle Roberts

Doctor Benedict Lowell ran his hands through his overly long black hair and adjusted his small, wire-rimmed glasses. "I'm impressed. Poor Percy always said you were a fine engineer, and I knew you were clever, but I underestimated how gifted you truly are. Your schematic is beautiful. Your theory is novel, yet sound. Capturing the electrical energy of the human body is a brilliant idea and I doubt a man would have come up with such a perfect instrument to do the job. We tend to think large and flashy, but a generator as small as a clock, so each family might power their own home, is more workable." He picked up her clumsy prototype and tapped the energy-storage indicator, which currently read EMPTY. "I know you said your model didn't work consistently, but all your formulae seem correct. I suspect the problem lies in construction, not design."

Claire laughed. "I'm far better at designing devices than I am at building them. I came to arcane engineering as an adult. I wasn't encouraged to tinker in the basement as boys are. And the laboratories at Wellesley are unsophisticated compared to this." She gestured around her old friend's lab in the arcane engineering department at the Massachusetts Institute of Technology, a veritable paradise of devices both mechanical and magical to aid engineers in their work.

Doctor Lowell opened the back of the device and peered at her handiwork. "Perhaps using silk instead of horsehair with the human hair...and certainly some of the gears need to be rendered smaller. A homunculus is invaluable in such delicate work, with its tiny hands that can fit where ours cannot. I fear the women's colleges are not well equipped with automatons as we are at MIT." His eyes gleamed with a pleasure Claire recognized, the pleasure of a scientist confronted with an intriguing problem. "I can help turn your mock-up into a working device, Mrs. Fitzwilliams."

"*Professor* Fitzwilliams," Claire corrected automatically and without rancor. As one of the first women in America to become a professor of arcane engineering she was used to the error. Even her students at Wellesley, young ladies who themselves aspired to become arcane engineers, sometimes forgot. She could hardly be angry with Doctor Lowell for slipping up, not when he had known her while her husband was still alive and she had been conducting her researches privately with Percy, not teaching.

And not when he had lovely blue eyes and a full, sensual mouth, currently smiling at her. As a widowed professor at a ladies' college, Claire had to appear a model of propriety lest her students' parents question her influence on their daughters, but that lab explosion had taken poor Percy from her more than five years ago and she was lonely. It was only natural to enjoy a handsome man's smile. "Excellent. My undergraduates are helpful for simpler projects, but this is too advanced for them."

Not to mention it was the sort of project that would get her fired if word got back to the administration.

"Your letter asking for my help said only that the device uses the energy of the human body to power itself. You said you would be more specific when we met. I verified that it should work as you theorized; not only will it, but if it proves suitable for mass production, it could bring electricity to the most isolated homestead. But does it gather all the energy we generate in a day, or something more specific? Do you envision it sitting in a workshop, or in the kitchen as a housewife does her chores? Maybe a schoolyard? Children at play are certainly energetic."

Now came the part she'd most dreaded when envisioning this meeting. On one hand, her plan would use a form of energy that was wasted otherwise—and one in unlimited supply. On the other hand, the particulars were delicate, especially to discuss with such an attractive man.

Claire schooled herself not to blush. "It gathers the yearnings of the unmarried and the unhappily married and converts all that heat into useful form while—in theory, once I get it working properly—easing a lonely person's restlessness."

If only she could get it to work for her. Her empty widow's bed was driving her mad with loneliness, but most men didn't wish to have a tinkering, teaching wife, and she lacked both time and patience for the niceties of courtship. "To sell it, we'd have to refer to something vague like 'electrical impulses inherent to the adult human body,' so as not to cause scandal."

Doctor Lowell stood and leaned across his great oak desk, an aggressive move that brought him closer than propriety allowed.

It was closer than Claire's own sense of propriety could combat. He loomed close enough that his aftershave filled her nostrils, layered over a scent that could only be the muskiness

of an aroused man—not the same as her late husband's, but
close enough to make her heart pound against her corset boning
and awaken neglected, intimate parts of her body. She ached,
yearning for touch, for kisses, for caresses; for, to be frank, a
man in her arms, a man's prick inside her.

She forced the thoughts away. It was impossible for her, as
for so many in this world of rigid rules, to enjoy such pleasures anymore. But that was the value of her invention. If
Doctor Lowell would help her construct it, there would be no
shortage of fuel for it, and people's longings could light their
lamps instead of giving them the vapors or prompting them to
do things they'd regret later.

Things such as kissing Doctor Lowell, which seemed like a
far better idea than Claire knew it was.

"No, Professor Fitzwilliams," Lowell said, his voice pitched
to a low, intimate whisper. "I cannot assist you with making a
device designed to harness the energy of sexual frustration. It
wouldn't be right."

Claire had anticipated this argument. The fact that it could
be distressing to be single or widowed, that one might long for
pleasures not readily or safely available, wasn't discussed in
polite society. But her invention had so much potential—could
do so much real good—that breaking that silence was necessary.
"I realize it's a taboo area, but you, as a man of science, must
know that right and wrong transcend convention. Is it right
that the air in our cities is black from coal smoke? My brother
is a physician and he fears that as we find more uses for electrical and steam power and burn more coal to generate it, lung
complaints will increase. Is it right that miners risk their lives
to acquire that coal?" She reached into her automated reticule,
grabbed a newspaper and snapped it down in front of Lowell.
"Only this week a dozen miners were killed in Kentucky. Four

of them were mere boys. Is it *right* that such tragedies must continue when arcane engineering has the potential to harness the energy inherent in the human body?" She rose to her feet, unwilling to stay seated and appear cowed.

"So passionate..." he murmured, "but confound it, Mrs. Fitzwilliams... Professor...Claire. Can't you see that your passion is why working on this device with you wouldn't be right? Your husband was like my little brother. And I am without a wife, a fiancée, or even, since we are speaking frankly, a mistress. You are the sort of woman I find intriguing, with your combination of beauty and intellect. Even when Percy was alive I found it hard to be near you without thinking things one shouldn't think about the wife of a close friend. Or anyone else's wife, for that matter. And now you come to me with this erotic device and ask for my aid. Do you mean to torture me?" He pounded his fist on the desk.

A hot flush started somewhere around Claire's suddenly slick privates and no doubt mottled her bosom before reaching her cheeks. "Doctor Lowell..." Surely it was all right to call an old acquaintance by his first name when he had just declared love, or at least enduring desire and infatuation? "Ben, I'm sorry. I had no wish to distress you. I knew you were fond of me and I knew I could trust you. That was my only thought, I swear." *At least it was my only thought before I actually saw you again. I adored Percy, but if I had met you first, I'm not sure he would have stood a chance. You and Percy were equals in intellect, but he was a charming boy to the end, where you are a handsome, well-built man.*

"I know you meant no harm," Doctor Lowell said. "And I agree with what you say. As we develop more uses for electricity and steam, we'll need cleaner ways to generate power or progress will cause more problems than it solves. Your notion of capturing and magnifying our own energy has great potential. Unfortunately, I can't do this work with you. Not if I want to keep my sanity and you your virtue. If you give me the plans, I'll build the device for you." He sighed. "Certainly I shall be frustrated enough to test it just thinking that you are behind the blueprint."

No! She wanted to be involved in this great work, not hand it off. Ben was too honorable to take credit, but if she wasn't there in the lab by his side, those skeptical of women scientists would assume he was the inventor, she a mere assistant who drew up the plans from his notes. "Perhaps I can modify the plans with your help. Even the energy of a person moving about, walking from place to place, could be captured. The power source does not need to be something so risqué. It would certainly be more acceptable to the public were it not."

"More acceptable, but less powerful. Sexual desire is one of humanity's strongest impulses, and all the stronger for being repressed. You hit on a potential solution to energy generation, one far cleaner and safer than coal. But not safer for me, Claire...not as long as you're behind it."

Ben stepped out from behind his worktable.

Even through the concealment of his lab coat, Claire could see his erection straining at the buttons of his wool trousers. (Trousers with burn holes in them, she noted, just like Percy's always had.) He moved like some great, wild-maned predator, all power and grace, his eyes intent on her.

She backed away.

But not to escape.

She should leave, give them both a chance to clear their heads. Ben was a gentleman and a friend, but desire could incinerate such niceties as common sense and proper behavior toward a lady, let alone a lady who was also a colleague.

She knew this because desire was making her forget good sense, good manners and the prudish behavior expected of female arcane engineers working in a man's world. She and Percy had enjoyed excellent marital relations, but she couldn't remember ever reaching this wet, trembling, fevered state from just a look and some suggestive words.

Then again, perhaps that was what happened when several years of excellent marital relations came to an abrupt, tragic end. The human body ran on electrical impulses, and if some of those impulses were repeatedly sparking without an outlet, one was bound to become a bit combustible.

Natural science could explain why the look in Ben's eyes was enough to set Claire's embroidered silk drawers on fire.

It also explained that female and male beasts were naturally drawn together to mate. Mr. Darwin had proved to Claire's scholarly satisfaction that humans, at least physically, were merely beasts with big brains.

Just because she and Ben Lowell had particularly large brains didn't make them above the physical. This was just natural science in action, and she might be an arcane engineer, but she had to respect the laws of natural science.

Instead of bolting toward the door like a decent woman should, Claire backed up so she was leaning against a sturdy table, empty except for a few spare gears and a small orrery.

Ben caught her there and wrapped his arms around her. She didn't pretend to resist, just turned up her face to meet the kiss she knew was coming.

Ben didn't bother with a delicate, romantic start like Percy always had. There was something of the Lothario in the way he cupped her face firmly in his hand and opened her lips, and something of the ravening beast in the way he fell on her mouth and devoured it.

It awakened a ravening beast Claire hadn't known was within her. Heat surged from her lips throughout her body, zinging to her nipples and her sex.

The heat surged into her brain as well, reminding her how much she'd always admired Ben, how he would be able, like Percy and unlike most of the men she'd met since Percy's death, to stimulate her mind as well as her body.

She pressed her hips forward, thrilling to feel his hardness pressing against the juncture of her legs. There was too much fabric in the way, but the shock of contact still weakened her knees and made her moan out loud.

Ben pulled away abruptly. "Claire, leave before we do something foolish."

"What if I want to do something foolish? What if I told you I want to be bare as the day I was born in your arms?"

"I'd get hard—which I already was, but I swear your words just made me harder. My brain would seize up, too busy thinking of the things I want to enjoy with you to remember propriety and convention and all the reasons we shouldn't." Ben put his arms around her again, but seemed uncertain whether he should pull her closer or push her away. "But I'd have to try. Not because I want to resist, but because I'm too fond of you to risk your good name and your place in society."

"I'm sick of frustration, sick of propriety, sick of worrying about my good name!" She hadn't known how vehemently she felt about it until she began to speak, but five years of silence, shattered, let loose a torrent of words that surprised her as she spoke them. "Society other than that of other engineers means little to me, and I suspect it means even less to you. We've defied convention simply to become arcane engineers. A man faces challenges when his work's so little understood, and I don't need to tell you it's harder for a woman. So why should we stand on convention now? I like you and I want you, and you feel the same, so why shouldn't we be naked right now?"

A broad, sexy grin spread across Ben's face. "Some of my graduate students have keys to the laboratory. It would be better if we kept most of our clothes on in case of interruption, so we could at least pretend we hadn't been fucking against the worktable. Because I intend to fuck you against the worktable, Claire. Then I intend to take you home and do it again in a proper bed where we can be naked." He pulled her close again, and the ravening beast was back in his eyes. "You're right, of course. We don't need to stand on convention. I will help you with your device—and with your frustration and loneliness, if you'll help me with mine."

He drew her into another intense kiss, his hands running over her breasts. The sensible blue serge of her walking suit felt like the thinnest silk, she was so sensitized.

He was hard, so hard and so sexy in his lab coat, his hair mussed, his goggles still hanging around his neck where he'd put them when she arrived for her appointment. His hands were hot and strong, and even through all the confounded clothes she was obliged to wear to go about in society, he seemed to reach all the places she needed him to reach.

Then it was her turn to explore. His lab coat's texture was familiar to her fingers, because she wore one herself, but the cool cotton of a man's shirt felt alien after so long. She could feel crisp hair underneath and shivered at the sensation. Percy had had blond hair as fine as a baby's and no hair on his chest, but she thought she'd enjoy feeling Ben's furriness against her bare skin.

Her hand slipped down to his trouser fly, and before she had done more than touch the first button at his waistband, Ben groaned with pleasure and pressed forward against her hand.

She could think of no reason not to run her hand along his length through the tweed. "Lovely," she murmured. It didn't seem right to compare him to Percy. But she couldn't help thinking that he seemed thicker than Percy, if a bit shorter—and that such a shape would have merits.

She began working on the buttons of his fly with fingers that eagerness and tension made thick and clumsy. "I could use your homunculus right now," she joked, "with those little, agile hands."

"No," Ben said through gritted teeth. "I want to be inside you so badly, but I wouldn't hurry this. I've wanted you so long, Claire. So long."

"I think I must have wanted you without knowing it. Why else would I have come to you with a project that forced me to speak of sex?" Now that she let herself admit it, she'd always thought him attractive, but she'd loved Percy too much to let the thoughts go beyond aesthetic pleasure.

But would she have put her prettiest drawers on under her sensible walking suit if in the back of her mind, she hadn't dreamed of their meeting going like this; if she hadn't wanted to release his prick from the confines of his trousers and test its weight and length in her hand, studying it as carefully as she might some curious artifact or arcane component?

If she hadn't wanted to sink to her knees on the chemical-scorched laboratory floor and pull his heated length into her mouth?

If she hadn't wanted to taste his musk, to savor that salty tang that hinted at how delicious his spunk would be, to feel him pull the combs from her hair and tangle his fingers in its liberated weight as she ran her tongue along the silky length of his cock, teased at the head, then took him deep into her mouth again?

"God, it's been too long...if you don't..." She understood

Ben's broken words. She just wasn't sure she cared. She ached to feel him deep inside her, his body moving against hers, but at the same time, she didn't want to stop what she was doing. It had been a long time for her as well, too long. She'd willed herself to forget how good a man could taste and how powerful a woman could feel on her knees, were she on her knees willingly in order to drive a man to distraction.

And she'd forgotten—if she'd even known, with gentle Percy—how good it felt when a man directed her sucking, or how insanely wonderful it felt when he lost patience and pulled her abruptly to her feet, reeling her in for another devastating kiss.

Then Ben turned her around to lean against the table, his movements made rough by eagerness. He flipped up her skirt and stroked her sex through her silk drawers.

His fingers, so clever at building inventions, were equally clever at teasing her. He circled her clit perfectly. Pressure built low in her belly. Her head swam with need. Without thinking about it, she began moving her hips, creating a rhythm along with his fingers.

"Talk about...the energy of the human body," she managed to say.

Then she lost her ability for coherent speech. Her hips danced and bucked. She gripped the hard surface of the table. As the first orgasm not of her own furtive making she'd enjoyed since Percy died wracked her body, she bit into her own sleeve to stifle a scream.

Then, and only then, did he pull her drawers down. She stepped out of them and kicked them aside.

One finger slid into her.

God, it felt huge. Huge and wonderful. "I think I'm as tight again as I was on my wedding night. Only I'm much wetter, because I know how glorious it will be."

"Wet, but not wet enough. Wait here." She heard him rummaging in his desk. When he came back, he had a most curious object in his hand. One long tube of brass had a gear mechanism on its end, and connected to it, a ball of what appeared to be hard rubber. Gears and a small glass tube on the side of the second attached tube marked it as a clockwork, but she couldn't figure out its purpose. More to the point, she couldn't figure out why Ben had chosen this instant to show off a new invention. "I want to see your work, but later. Talking science in the afterglow is fine, but I can't concentrate now."

He chuckled in a way that caressed her sex as much as his hands had earlier. Then he whispered a word she couldn't quite make out, but it was definitely Latin.

One of those devices then, the kind with clockworks powered not by electricity or simple mechanics, but by a tiny animus or spirit who provided the energy in exchange for the chance to observe the human world. Despite her arousal, her engineer's curiosity was also aroused. "A spirit drive? Have you found a way to make the creature stay? They're not the most reliable power source. Spirits get bored too easily."

"I've summoned a minor incubus. I can guarantee he won't be bored, not with you open and slick and needy before him."

She thought he was joking. Arcane engineers didn't work with incubi, as a rule, since the creatures were not only flighty, but prone to escaping the devices and provoking any female in the area.

Then he touched the device to her clit.

He hadn't been joking. Only an incubus could power a device that spun and whirred and teased like this one did—and oh, god, had an appendage that thrust out from the second tube and into her, into her like she hoped Ben would do himself very, very soon.

Only an incubus could power such a device. And only a twisted genius could invent it in the first place.

"Percy and I designed this together as a lark," he said.

Make that two twisted geniuses.

"I always told him he should take it home and try it on you, but he feared you'd be offended he'd invent such a thing and even more offended that we'd worked on it together."

"I'll be offended," she managed to say, "if you turn it off."

Then she stopped talking and started screaming, "Oh, god, oh, god. Ben...this thing...oh, god."

The orgasm, when it came, ripped through her entire body and lasted longer than she dreamed possible.

But it still wasn't enough. Her need for release was sated, but the orgasm-by-device only heightened her need for physical contact.

"Please," she said, pushing her bottom back at Ben. "Please."

"Should I call the incubus back?" he asked, even while he ran the head of his prick over her needy sex. "Get the device powered up again?"

"No...you. Please, I need you."

"I thought you'd never ask."

He gripped her hips hard, hard enough that she imagined the bruises and the way they'd bring back memories of this day, and drove into her with a force that slammed her into the table.

This meant more bruises, but she didn't care. She pushed back against him, gave as good as she took, let loose five years of constrained desire.

And maybe longer than that, because now that she was fucking in a laboratory bent over a table and not particularly caring if someone walked in, now that she had been pushed to climax by a brilliant incubus-driven clockwork, all of Claire's inhibitions shattered. Sex and science mingled too perfectly to resist.

She screamed, she beat on the table with her fist, she begged for more, she moved any way she could think of to get that fine, fat prick deeper inside her.

She came more often than she'd ever imagined she could.

It couldn't last long, not at that pace, but by the time Ben let out a great cry and surged into her, Claire could barely hold herself up.

"Grab your things," he muttered.

"Don't want to move."

"My lodgings aren't far from here, and my bed is far more comfortable than this table. Do you need to get back to Wellesley tonight, my dear?"

"No classes until Monday." She was moving in a daze, picking up her papers and tucking them back into their leather notebook, finding her drawers and stuffing them into the reticule along with the notebook since putting them back on seemed like far too much trouble. She set the reticule to follow after her. She wanted to hold hands with Ben without either of them struggling with the reticule.

"Good. I don't intend to let you out of my bed until Sunday. Although perhaps we should look for a justice of the peace."

She stopped in her tracks.

Ben circled the desk and embraced her again. "Neither of us may care about convention, but colleges tend to fire you if you're unmarried and living together. And I want you to have access to the laboratory here, which you could as my wife. I bet we could get your device…"

He glanced at the desk and his voice filled with awe. "Claire, your device is working now. The battery is full." He unplugged his electric lamp and plugged it into the socket on the device. It lit up. "It needed fulfillment and pleasure to power it, not frustration."

She threw her arms around him. "I'll marry you, if only to stop paying the power company. I'm sure we can light up the whole of Cambridge, let alone one home. But I have to figure out where the calculations are awry. We could never sell something like this; it's far too risqué. Besides there are far more lonely people than fulfilled ones."

"But imagine what we could do if we packaged your generator and my toy together and sold them as wedding gifts? Plenty of bright, warm, happy homes. The coal barons would be out of business in no time."

He kissed her again, tenderly this time.

THE SERVANT QUESTION

Janine Ashbless

Picture, if you will, a room that looks rather like the salon of a high-class dressmaker's or milliner's establishment. There are tall windows to allow the best possible light to fall upon the merchandise being displayed; there is a low stage; there are drapes and Grecian columns and a large potted fern. Picture, too, a lady of the most respectable class seated in an armchair before the dais, and standing beside her the figure of Mr. Edward Tulliver, sporting a neatly trimmed moustache, a finely tailored suit and the forthright air of a man at the pinnacle of his profession. This is the showroom of Tulliver's Mechanical Servants.

"It is such a problem keeping good staff," complained Mrs. Petherton, whose husband was a rising star in the Foreign and Extratellurian Office. Having seen the apparatus Mr. Tulliver had on offer and witnessed an impressive demonstration of it at work, she was in a mood to confide. "We had a very reasonable scullery maid—a mousey little thing, wouldn't say 'Boo' to a goose, you would have thought—and only last month she left to become, of all things, a hostess on the P&O Mars Dirigible. I understand she appears nightly in the most alarming feather headdress. It's almost beyond comprehension."

"Quite," said Mr. Tulliver, who could only aspire to Mrs. Petherton's social status and, having built his own enterprise from the foundations of his father's watch-making business, might have had rather more empathy with a scullery maid's stifled ambition than her erstwhile employer did. He did not see it as his place to argue, however: Mrs. Petherton was a valued customer. Moreover she was still, despite the imminent arrival of her middle years, a most handsome and well-proportioned woman whose personal charm was considerable. As susceptible as any of his gender, he felt no desire to dismay in any way the possessor of such a fine figure, or such bright eyes. So he said soothingly; "I hear complaints such as yours from every quarter, madam. The civilized world is crying out for hard-working, diligent and above all reliable domestics. Which is precisely why we offer such a service, here at Tulliver's Mechanical Servants."

"And then there was Mrs. Leatherby," she continued, unstoppable, flashing those brilliant eyes as she blinked in disbelief at the recollection. "I mean... Really! French trained, and quite the best cook we'd had. My husband always said he had never tasted a better mutton joint than hers. She went off to work for the director of the Sub-Atlantic Rail Project. I mean to say...an American! What do they know of dining? It will be only steak and chipped potatoes with him, I don't doubt."

Her magnificent bosom heaved under its white lawn blouson, and she dabbed at her upper lip with a lace handkerchief. Mr. Tulliver decided it was politic to move the conversation in a more positive direction.

"But you are quite content with your Tulliver Automated Chef, are you not, madam?"

Mrs. Petherton inclined her head. "Yes, indeed. Very content. I had my doubts, Mr. Tulliver, when you first installed it. I don't mind telling you that."

"Madam, an attitude of proper caution can only be to your credit. Yet I hope we have earned your trust now?"

"Certainly, six months without being pestered for a rise in wages is quite a novelty. My husband grumbles that the food has not the same flare as Cook brought to it, but I daresay it is only bluster. He certainly always has second helpings."

Mr. Tulliver waved a hand at the figure that stood motionless upon the dais. "And I am sure that you will find the Tulliver Tireless Housemaid of equal value in the domestic realm, madam, should you choose to make a purchase. As the notices in the newspapers say: 'Every home should have a Tulliver!'"

The object of his praise, which had already demonstrated its capacity for dusting an armoire full of Dresden crockery and folding a pile of bed linen, was decidedly feminine in form but no more organic in nature than a grandfather clock. Dressed in housemaid's black and white, it had a pretty porcelain face and jointed enamel fingers. Under its little white cap its hair was a solid piece of molded brass. Even at rest, the whir of its complex clockwork innards was faintly audible, like the purr of a cat.

Mrs. Petherton stood up with a decisive action, smoothing down her skirt, and approached the maid. The expression on her face was one of cautious fascination. "You say she can take instruction?"

"The Tireless Housemaid is designed to obey your voice and has a number of domestic routines already implanted. It is capable of adapting these to different room layouts and sizes." The salesman's words spilled smoothly off Tulliver's tongue. "If there are specific tasks which you wish it to perform that are not already in its repertoire, you can call myself or one of my staff out at any time to adjust the mechanism and implant a new routine. We pride ourselves upon our unparalleled service to our customers."

"Can she talk?"

"I confess, madam, that this model does not—beyond a simple vocal signal of 'Yes, ma'am,' or 'Yes, sir,' upon acknowledgement of your instructions. However, we hope to produce a fully conversant model next year, and if you should at that point like to change up to the new version, we would see to it at once."

Mrs. Petherton thrust her lower lip out most becomingly. "Actually, I believe I would prefer the silent version." She looked the maid up and down, and her eyebrows arched as she took in the pinched waist and the swell of the hips. "Tell me...underneath..."

"Madam?"

"Beneath...her clothes. There's nothing beastly, is there?"

"Please, madam." Mr. Tulliver drew himself upright, though he well remembered nights in the workshop molding those porcelain buttocks to aesthetically perfect curves. "Let me assure you, Tulliver's Tireless Housemaids are sold only to lady customers. No aspersions may be cast upon our products. In fact, it is yet another advantage of having automated servants rather than the traditional variety. There are no inclinations to waywardness in the clockwork heart. "

Mrs. Petherton nodded. "Quite. Well." She smiled and turned back to him, with an unconscious lift of her bosom that Mr. Tulliver found somewhat distracting. "I shall call her Eliza, I believe."

In the weeks that followed, Mr. Tulliver called at the Petherton town house in Grosvenor Square several times. Each was the occasion of a small frisson of pride for him, for he remembered accompanying his father to just such exalted dwellings as a small boy, and in those days Tullivers senior and junior had been expected to present themselves at the servants' door. Now, such were the times and such was Edward Tulliver's rise in the world, that his customers regarded it as a positive cachet for him to be seen alighting at their front entrance. It put the Pethertons at the very vanguard of fashionable society to have a Tulliver Tireless Housemaid at their disposal, and the ladies of their social circle were eager to order their own versions of the indefatigable Eliza. The fact that such an apparatus had to be individually crafted to order made them eager to court his favor and dispense with the usual social formalities.

From Mr. Tulliver's point of view, then, the visits were not begrudged. Every time he breathed the air of the Pethertons' drawing room he felt his heart thrill as with the promise of a spring morning. Despite his ordinary background, he had always longed for the day when he would be accepted among the higher echelons. How assiduously he had worked to delete the accent and manners of the artisan class, in preparation for this moment! How wonderful it was to take tea with ladies, who were, he felt, imbued by their delicate breeding with a special beauty and grace. He had always desired their admiration and now their social intercourse—the wide-eyed questions, the tinkling laughter—stiffened his resolve.

He looked forward to the day when there would be a Tireless Housemaid in all the finest homes, and he would be just as familiar with all the grandames of society.

Thus, every time he added a new routine to Eliza's repertoire, he felt again the pride that Michelangelo must have felt at his labors upon the Sistine Chapel: the pride of the true artist who brings something unique and incomparable to a discerning and exalted employer. Eliza seemed more beautifully wrought each time he visited, both more lifelike and more inhumanly perfect. Perhaps this was because her new owner had had her dressed in a fine uniform, complete with all the layers of undergarments so necessary to the soft feminine form—and so unnecessary in Eliza's case. To open the panel at her back involved Mr. Tulliver partially undressing her: undoing a myriad of buttons and loosening the tight stays and delving beneath the layers of lavender-scented frillies. The mannequin was so lifelike in form that this actually brought a blush to his cheek, as if he really were undressing a servant girl in front of her mistress. He was always sure to close the curtains before starting, in case some passerby should glimpse the operation and misunderstand.

"Mr. Tulliver, I do believe you are becoming an expert on the mysteries of the female undergarment," Mrs. Petherton teased him gently from the sofa, as he pulled out the crossed laces of the Housemaid's corset and wriggled the boned garment down to her porcelain hips.

In the glass over the mantle, Eliza's perfectly formed lips seemed to smile at him. Her ceramic breasts were pert and unyielding under her chemise.

"I assure you, madam," he answered jocularly, feeling the heat rise behind his tight collar, "that after the complexities of such apparel, the mere workings of a thousand interlocking clockwork cogs is as nothing."

In point of fact Mrs. Petherton's requirements of Eliza were exacting and particular, and the new maid had to be implanted with the precise techniques for several new chores. The beating of carpets, for example, seemed to be a task not to be undertaken with brute force but with measured blows and a particular upward flick of the wrist that Mrs. Petherton insisted was superior for driving out dust; not having personal experience of domestic chores, Mr. Tulliver could only assume that this was derived from the store of feminine wisdom. The polishing of champagne flutes (two fingers inside and a twisting motion of the wrist) caused him some small trouble with the minute adjustments to Eliza's mechanism, but Mrs. Petherton pronounced herself very pleased with the results. Then there was the occasion he was summoned to improve the housemaid's technique with the dolly-tub. Mr. Tulliver considered that anything that took the backbreaking work of pounding laundry out of human hands must be an improvement, but apparently that too had its particular techniques that he had not foreseen. To optimize efficiency, according to Mrs. Petherton, Eliza must employ a back and forth motion of the hips whilst working the dolly-stick.

It was, though he would not let on, all valuable information to Mr. Tulliver. He had assumed that housework would be quite simple, and upon discovering otherwise he was grateful to be able to refine his automatons' routines.

So he was neither terribly surprised nor particularly put out when, one afternoon, a telegram was delivered asking him to come to the Petherton residence at his earliest convenience, as Eliza needed yet more adjustment. Mr. Tulliver donned his hat and caught a hansom without delay; he was pulling the bell chain within a quarter of an hour. A middle-aged housemaid— a human one, for Eliza was not capable of complex social interactions—opened the door and admitted him.

"Good afternoon, Charlotte. Is Mrs. Petherton at home?"

"Ma'am said you were to go right through to the drawing room, sir," she told him, indicating the passageway. He was a little surprised that she didn't precede him to announce his arrival, and after a few steps he half turned and glanced back. The maid was staring after him with the most peculiar expression on her face, lips tightly pursed and eyebrows arched. Mr. Tulliver hurried away, feeling a little flustered. He was aware that the servant class resented his work, which they saw—quite rightly—as having the potential to drive down their wages and put them out of employment. He could only interpret that face as expressing a marked disapproval.

Just what it was that she disapproved of, however, was something that was to take him by surprise. When he tapped upon the drawing room door and let himself in, he was confronted by a sight that seemed to have stepped from the most fevered of imaginations. For a moment he wondered if he were dreaming.

"Oh, Mr. Tulliver!" gasped Mrs. Petherton. "Thank Heaven you are here!"

The Angel of the House was arranged upon hands and knees upon the chaise lounge in a state of some dishabille, for her dress seemed to have been discarded on the hearthrug and she was clad only in her drawers, chemise and corset—and indeed seemed to be spilling voluptuously out of all three. The rosy globes of her behind were peeking through the split in her drawers. Directly behind her stood Eliza, also stripped down to her undergarments, although in the case of the automaton the porcelain flesh revealed was neither flushed nor damp with sweat nor wobbling wildly. Secured about Eliza's hips was an arrangement of black leather straps, and from them protruded the jutting shape of a huge ebony phallus with which she was plundering the hole of her mistress, moving with a steady, forceful—and yes, Tireless—rocking motion of her jointed hips.

"Madam!" said Mr. Tulliver faintly, as all the blood deserted his head.

Eliza smiled serenely, as her hips thrust back and forth and her hands jerked an invisible dolly-stick.

"Oh, Mr. Tulliver, you must aid me," Mrs. Petherton

groaned. "She has been at work for some time, as you can see, but her technique is sadly ineffective!"

"Ineffective?" Mr. Tulliver tugged at his collar with something like desperation: it seemed to be constricting his throat. That would account for the blankness of his normally swift mind.

Mrs. Petherton stamped her knuckles into the fabric of the chaise longue, pushing back onto the phallus and wriggling her hips. Her face was most fetchingly pink, he noted, and her hair was escaping from its careful chignon. "I cannot reach the climactic state I desire!" she wailed.

Mr. Tulliver cleared his throat. "I see," he managed to say. "Well, perhaps..."

"Please, Mr. Tulliver! You cannot imagine my frustration. Act swiftly, I implore you!"

"Ahem. Yes." He shut the door and approached across the Persian carpet, fumbling at his bag of tools, feeling his own heart hammering like a steam pump. From a little to the rear he had a very fine view indeed of the straps cinched about Eliza's thighs and bottom, their dark leather contrasting beautifully with the snowy white linen of her undergarments; of the thick, contoured phallus, lacquered and shiny with Mrs. Petherton's feminine juices, plunging in and out of her tight hole; of the soft brown intimate hair and the stretched, pink flesh, riven by the invader. He could smell the hot bouquet of her excitement and it seemed to him more invigorating than the sweetest engine oil.

"I see." His voice was gravelly, but—he hoped—confident. Beneath his own clothes his prick was stiff and throbbing with an ardent urgency, bidding to rival the artificial limb so hard at work before him, but his professional instinct mastered the carnal one. "Pray tell, madam: is the...ahem...piston of sufficient girth?"

"It fits very well, Mr. Tulliver."

"And is the, um, penetration deep enough?"

"It is, Mr. Tulliver."

He nodded. "There seems to be effective lubrication of the intersecting parts. Then perhaps her motions are somehow insufficiently diverse. Let me see what I can do." As quickly as he could he loosened Eliza's stays and tugged open her garments to reveal her back panel. His hands were trembling as he struggled with the clothes, but as soon as he had a screwdriver between his fingers they grew steady. He flipped the panel open and surveyed the whirring mechanism within. "She is currently performing a linear thrusting motion. Perhaps if we try this..."

A tiny but expert adjustment of the mechanism induced a shift in Eliza's hips. Mrs. Petherton cried out, conveying that the sensations in her nether parts were now recognizably different.

"Yes?" he asked.

"Oh, yes! Get her to do that again!"

"Hmm. A simple to-and-fro motion does not seem adequate. Yet in combination with..." His fingers danced upon the brass work, making minute changes to the clockwork motion.

"Oh, yes, oh, yes!" cried Mrs. Petherton, most gratifyingly.

"Splendid. I think a figure-eight roll of the hips seems to work well."

Mrs. Petherton concurred, calling upon the Almighty to bear witness to the improvement in her lot. She seemed even more pleased when he got Eliza to grip her hip with one hand and slap her generously proportioned bottom with the other. Her flesh bounced and jiggled as inanimate matter pounded her with unfailing vigor. Mr. Tulliver slipped his screwdrivers back into their pouch and stood back, surveying the scene critically. He was an artisan, never able to resist tinkering: now that his expertise had been brought into play he wanted to explore all the parameters. His fingers, trained in the finest engineering workshops of England, were well used to greasing nipples and tightening nuts. Now, with an absorbed frown, he reached underneath Mrs. Petherton to flick the little button of feminine flesh that so effectively acts as ignition to a woman's inner fires.

Mrs. Petherton panted and groaned, her eyes closed, her face red, her teeth bared.

Mr. Tulliver was pleased with his experiment and repeated it just to be sure, while Eliza pumped and ground into her mistress from behind. But his professional curiosity extended further. Moving down her body he scooped out her glorious breasts from her corset, letting their prodigious weight fall into his hands. The silk of her chemise was plastered to her skin with the sweat of her exertions. Her nipples were big and rosy and it turned out—when he pinched and tugged them—exquisitely sensitive.

"Oh, yes!" gasped Mrs. Petherton. She was quite magnificent in her beauty and her ardor, he thought—and almost as tireless as Eliza. But he sensed she would not be able to hold out for much longer. His own agitation was rising to a peak too; one that demanded decisive action.

"Madam," he said, unbuttoning his trousers and manhandling his stiff prick out into view. "If you would be so kind..." So saying, he made bold to insert it between her open lips. Mrs. Petherton's raised eyebrows signaled her surprise but any protests at his forwardness were muffled and inaudible. Indeed, within moments she was sucking upon it obligingly, her hot wet mouth slurping upon him as he ground her teats between his knuckles, her gasps escaping now around his thick shaft. So primed was the engine of her desire by the previous labors of the Tireless Housemaid that, in very short order, she yielded to both nature and artifice and spent ecstatically, her shuddering paroxysms testifying to her transport as her throat engulfed him to the root.

Without warning she pulled away from Mr. Tulliver's prick. Its rubicund head popped from between her lips, slicked with her saliva. "Eliza, rest!" she gasped, and the mannequin froze.

"Mrs. Petherton," he stammered, gripping his shaft, trying desperately to master himself as a gentleman should. "Madam, I am overcome—ah! My most sincere apologies." But it was too late: he was beyond recall, unable to stop himself. With a stroke of his wrist he let fly his tribute upon her enormous quivering breasts, his climax racked from him in electric spasms.

"Oh, my goodness, Mr. Tulliver!"

Mr. Tulliver watched, mesmerized, as his spend oozed down the snowy slopes of her bosom. He had never, he thought faintly, seen anything more wondrous.

"Mr. Tulliver!"

He shook himself. "Madam?"

Mrs. Petherton disengaged herself from Eliza and knelt upright on the seat. "I regret to tell you that I am not entirely satisfied with the Tulliver Tireless Housemaid."

"Oh...I, uh..."

"She has made a thorough mess down here." She thrust her fingers into the silky fleece of her intimate parts and spread them, revealing coral-colored lips that glistened with her juices. "And as yet you have not provided her with the apparatus to clean it up. Until she has a tongue in her head..."

"Madam," he said, sinking to his knees before her, "I am entirely at your disposal."

SLEIGHT
OF HAND

Renee Michaels

A prickle skittered over Cassie's skin, setting her a little on edge. It wasn't fear; it was anticipation. She loved the "seat of your pants" feeling rife with the possibility of getting caught.

The glint of the wide gold band through her tatted mitten caught her attention, and her loneliness surfaced. She really missed having a lover. Even platonic relationships proved to be restrictive in her line of work. She was an excellent thief but a dreadful liar. People tended to ask questions about her inexplicable absences, and besides, she despised having to explain herself.

Reaching up, Cassie checked to make sure the veil masking her face was in place, as were the shroud and the voluminous yards of bombazine and padding disguising her body. Who'd pay any attention to a widow when so many others bustled along the platform like a flock of black pouter pigeons?

Hand firmly gripping the valise that carried her tools, Cassie casually took her position by the private railway car in which the item she'd been commissioned to acquire was secured. She ran an experienced eye over the crowd, gauging the demeanor of the porters who kept an eye out for petty thieves who might be tempted to dip their sticky fingers into the pockets and reticules of the distracted passengers.

All the players were in place waiting for their cue.

Right on time, five minutes before departure, the whistle of the 10:35 train leaving Victoria Station for Bath issued a raucous blare, sending its passengers into a flurry of motion. The signal would set her plan in motion.

Kit, her accomplice, stepped out from behind a column a few feet from his target. With his sunny blond hair dulled by coal dust, face smeared with smut and his clothes with the requisite holes burnt into the cloth, he looked like a chimney sweep, as was their intention.

He darted through the crowd, grinning cheekily at the women who pulled back their full skirts to save them from the trail of black soot he left in his wake.

Nimbly, Kit clambered up the side of the steam engine and tossed several metal balls of varying thicknesses down the smoke stack. Some contained precisely measured amounts of gunpowder for loudness, others magnesium for bright flashes of light to erroneously magnify the danger of the explosions.

A short bleat from a whistle told her Kit had caught the porters' attention. He scampered down and, wily as a fox, evaded his pursuers and disappeared into the crowd, luring the authorities away.

Cassie began her countdown. The balls would melt at carefully calculated intervals and set off a series of explosions, giving her what she needed.

Chaos.

At the first blast, the crowd froze, then galvanized into action. They streamed from the trains like ants, screaming, clutching their children or the hands of a spouse. People dragged apart in the melee added to the hysteria. Shouts and screams, the pounding of shoe leather on brick added to the cacophony. A door behind her flew open and a well-dressed couple joined the panicked throng stampeding to the exits.

Cassandra waited exactly five heartbeats before she scampered up the short flight of stairs. The hourglass in her head began to mark time. She had twenty minutes between the first blast and the last, adding ten for the smoke to clear. That gave her exactly half an hour at the most to complete her task.

Having memorized the layout of the club car, she walked swiftly through the opulent sitting area to the rear compartment used as a study.

Always cautious, she pressed her ear to the door and listened: no sounds of movement from within the room. Wonderful. Turning the lever on the door, she grinned with satisfaction when it opened easily; three minutes saved because she wouldn't have to pick the lock. She almost did a jig in her glee.

Her objective dominated the snug room. Made of mahogany, the desk gleamed richly in the dim light. Not wasting any time, she dropped to her knees to study the locks on the safe box built into the side of the desk. Her exuberance died a swift death.

"Well, bollocks," Cassandra gritted out the vulgar bit of cant.

Stymied by a Fitzgibbon triple-slip lock, again. The dratted man's inventions were really getting to be an annoyance. However, if she were honest with herself, his work wasn't the root of her irritation with him. How was an enterprising fingersmith like herself supposed to make a living if he persisted in creating unpickable locks?

Two of the bolts secured the safe; if you picked one lock, a third latch slid into place. At all times a duo of steel bolts stood between the thief and his booty.

She'd encountered this lock with increasing frequency. That being the case, it was a good thing she was a resourceful woman. Everything had a weakness, and she exploited it.

Reaching into her valise, she took out an embossed nickel case and unlatched it to reveal several small glass ampoules nestled in indentations carved into the velvet padded wooden rack to prevent them from jostling. The transparent balls glistened iridescently in the dim room. They looked innocuous.

She hated using them; the glass was as thin as a soap bubble. One small miscalculation and their contents would eat through your flesh like leprosy. However, the fee for this enterprise would keep her family fed and housed for the rest of the year. Cassie used her thumbnail to ease out three of the lethal pellets.

Don't break, don't break, she prayed silently.

Careful not to touch the metal plate on the lock, she slipped them through the circular lower part of the keyhole. Cassie released the breath she hadn't realized she was holding and scrambled back when she heard the soft tinkle of the globules shattering. The acrid fumes wafted over to sting her eyes and nostrils as the sulfuric acid ate away at the inner workings of the lock. Blinking back her tears, she started to mark time again. A minute and a half was all the corrosive fluid needed.

Soft clapping from the far corner of the room sent her confidence plummeting into her stomach. She was caught like a mouse in a trap.

"I wondered if I'd find the clever bastard who found a way to dismantle my work." The deep bass of the familiar voice made her predicament even more dire. "I never imagined it'd be a shady lady."

Emotions long buried were resurrected. Her body shook as if she had a bad bout of ague. Hell, Marcus Fitzgibbon! Could things get any worse?

She dared not say a word. He'd recognize her voice in an instant.

Rising to her feet, Cassie turned to face her tormentor, her nemesis—her love.

He mustn't find out who she was, or what she did to survive.

Cassie took a surreptitious look at the door. With a little luck, she might just make it. Resting her hand on the back of the desk chair, she prepared to make her escape. If he lunged at her, one hard push would send it crashing into him, giving her a precious few additional seconds.

Her eyes fixed on Marc's, she sidled sideways in the direction of the exit, earning her a wolfish smile full of menace and dark promises of retribution.

Marcus slid the panel beside him to the side and pulled a concealed lever.

The solid double thunk of dead bolts sliding into place made her jump. She imagined that was what the peal of doom sounded like.

She stared at the door, discombobulated. What in heaven's name was she going to do now? Never faced with a scenario she couldn't wiggle her way out of before, her mind went blank for a moment.

The creak of leather pulled her attention back to Marcus. He rose to his feet and stalked across the Aubusson carpet, his long, lean face grim, with storm-dark gray eyes glaring at her, his large body bridling with rage. Marcus's longer-than-fashionable hair added to the savagery of his stance. Cassie took an involuntary step back.

Another foot and he'd loom over her. The manly scent of

him would envelop her and the memories would come flooding back: their fanatic lovemaking, when they couldn't get enough of each other, and their rancorous breakup.

Cassie looked around, frantic now. No, time, she had no time. Think, think, why couldn't she think? The window. There was a lone window open, letting in hot dusty air. Though no more than a foot square, it was the road to salvation.

Cassie fumbled for the reticule attached to her waist filled with photographer's flash power. She set her thumb on the pumice ball affixed to the clasp. It'd spark and ignite the phosphorescent chemicals, blinding him momentarily.

Marcus's eyes followed the movement of her hand. With a snarl, he lunged at her. She shoved the chair at him but he slapped it aside and sent it careening into the wall, where it bounced off the barrier to teeter drunkenly.

His hand gripped her wrist like a manacle. Before she could react, he ripped her hat and veil off her head. The pain from the steel pins ripping at her scalp was nothing compared to the shock and disillusionment on Marcus's face.

"Cassie, why?"

She lifted her chin proudly. "Why? You tossed me aside and you ask me why, Mr. Fitzgibbon?" What she surmised was regret flashed through his eyes, and he opened his mouth but no words came. "What I do and who I do it with is no longer any concern of yours."

The consternation leached from his face and icy fury hardened his features. "Where have you been hiding these last three years? How the hell could you resort to thievery, when you could have come to me if you needed additional funds?" She recognized that obdurate tone; like a dog with a bone, he wouldn't let go.

Cassie gave Marcus the cool sardonic smile she knew he

hated and felt a glimmer of satisfaction when a flicker of irritation tightened his face.

In the haughtiest voice she could muster, considering her situation, she drawled as if she weren't quaking inside, "Sir, I wouldn't touch a ha'penny of yours, and they'll be doing the quadrille in hell before I answer any questions. I suggest you turn me over to the Blue Bottles; we wouldn't want to extend our unhappy reunion."

His fist tightened on her wrist. "You've been hanging out with the lower classes, my dear, you've picked up their verbiage. No need to involve anyone in our domestic difficulties."

In a flash, he hooked his foot around her ankle and sent her tumbling back onto a chesterfield. Pinning her with his knee on her stomach, he pulled leather straps from the frame and tethered her arms and legs to the chaise.

"What on earth...?" Cassie expostulated.

His lips twisted. "Struggling would be a waste of energy. How did Henley know to contact you to steal from me?"

Cassie, humiliated by her position, seared him with a fulminating glare but didn't utter a word of protest. She wouldn't give him the satisfaction. "I haven't the faintest idea what you're blathering about."

"Let me spin you a tale. His lordship finds a missive arranging a meeting with her ladyship for delivery of a certain package. He finds out I own this private car, and the elderly groom mistakenly surmises I'm diddling his wife and plots his revenge. His valet overhears him arranging for the theft of the item from my safe. The servant passes this bit of information to her ladyship's maid, who he *is* diddling, by the way, and the faithful Abigail passes this on to her mistress—who rushed here to warn me." Marcus grinned smugly down at her as the sound of a groan slipped from her lips.

"You're a fine one to criticize my language. Diddling? Really!" Cassie scoffed.

"I suspect Lord Henley thought you'd find love letters or some such thing." Marcus strolled over to the desk, used a letter opener to slide the drawer open and lifted out a box. "Imagine his surprise if you had succeeded and handed him this." He lifted up a phallus-shaped object for her perusal.

Cassie frowned. "What on God's green earth is that?"

"It was your twenty-fifth birthday present. You weren't around to receive it. It's a clockwork cock."

Cassie's mouth dropped open. "You perfected it?" Her first interested reaction gave way to indignation. "That was my idea, and you were giving my present to another woman?"

Marcus flipped up her skirts, exposing the lower half of her body, and trailed his fingers over her skin. "So contrary. I see you still have a penchant for prancing about bare-assed." He laid the cool column on her stomach. "Imagine His Lordship's consternation if he'd realized he'd hired my wife as his cracksman."

"I'm no common thief." Cassie writhed under his touch.

"I really should send Henley a box of cigars as a gesture of gratitude. After all, he managed to help me get you where I want you. Naked, well almost, and soon to be needing this. You didn't take any of the toys I made for you, but I think you'll really like this one."

Cassie remembered the exact moment she'd challenged him to furnish her with an inexhaustible phallus. Spent after a bout of lovemaking, he'd called her insatiable, so she'd made her daring suggestion. Being Marcus, he'd set to do just that.

"Marcus, what's come over you?" She frowned at him; he really wasn't acting like himself. Cassie shifted uncomfortably under his all-encompassing gaze. "Let's talk about this sensibly."

"The time for sanity has come and gone. You've turned me into a bedlamite." Marcus sank to his knees and pressed a kiss on her mons, before he lifted his head to stare at her. He was flushed with desire and that lusty smirk, which always set her insides fluttering, spread across his face.

"Shall we play?"

Marcus stared into Cassie's furious, pale-skinned face surrounded by black tendrils escaping from her bun. If it were possible, the sparks from her pansy-blue eyes would incinerate him on the spot. He struggled to temper his elation with the fact that she'd proved to be the royal pain in his arse that had been plaguing him. He pressed his face into her stomach. He didn't want her to see any hint of neediness.

He'd never understood why the vivacious Cassandra Devore had taken to him. He was a bookish man, with ink stains on his fingers and linen more often than not. Diagrams and equations crowded his mind to the exclusion of all else, until Cassie.

She was his miracle; not once had she looked at him blankly when he droned on about his latest invention. Through her, his gray world became a spectrum of brilliant experiences.

"Let me go, Marcus, this has gone on long enough. I'm not in the mood for your histrionics." She heaved up her hips to dislodge him.

"Why should I? You're my wife—mine to take." The minute the words left his mouth, he knew it was the wrong thing to say.

She bristled under him, irritation radiated from her, but his frustrations bogged him down into a mire of confusion. He was at a loss as to how to deal with her. How did one apologize to a wife? Marcus was no good with words. Did he really need them, though? She always said he'd shown her how he felt every time he loved her.

Maybe, if he showed her with every sinew in his body how

he felt, he could convey his remorse and his love. It was illogical and had no basis in fact, but he was a desperate man, and he was out of options.

"I never imagined you were such a boor. Finally showing your true colors?" Cassie tossed the insult at him as only she could, sweetly scornful and accompanied by curled lips.

"No one knows me better than you. One misstep and you cut me completely out of your life," he declared gruffly. "You've punished me for my lack of faith long enough."

"You have not begun the sentence I've imposed on you. You accused me of spreading my legs like a Haymarket whore," she shrieked.

Marcus reared back as if she'd punched him. "I never called you a prostitute."

"You may as well have." She pursed her lips in a thin line, diminishing their enticing fullness.

"God's blood, Cass, what was I supposed to think? I saw what I believed was incontrovertible proof with my own eyes." The memory was as fresh as the day it had become etched in his mind. "You were half-naked, with the gadgets I fashioned for our personal pleasure scattered around you, and a strange man's hand on you shoulders."

"He was posing me. I was having an erotic portrait done for you, you cretin. Really, it was all the rage... But you took one look and left the room."

"A man can't think clearly when he's in a rage, it was either that or bloody commit murder. And I have no desire to swing at Tyburn."

"If our toys are so personal, why are you hawking them like a penny peddler to the likes of Lenora Henley?" At the moment, her feathers seemed to be more ruffled over the delivery of her toy, and he gladly latched on to the change of subject.

"Remember, you're the one who gave the faulty prototype to Monette Dupliss; she inquired if I'd improved on it." He paused at her condemning glare. "I needed to conduct trials on the dammed things, didn't I? She arranged for a few select women, known for their discretion, to...test them for me."

"How altruistic; of course there was nothing in it for you. All those women you helped to find pleasure, it was all for science of course. What a Banbury tale," she spat dismissively at his explanation.

"Christ Almighty! I'm done talking. There's no reasoning with you." He ripped off his morning coat, cravat and celluloid collar. They were strangling him, not to mention the constriction of his member by his trousers.

He fumbled with the ivory cameo at her throat, undid the row of buttons securing her bodice and parted the heavy material to reveal her torso.

His brows shot up when he caught sight of the thin black silk chemise. "Black?"

"I am after all a widow, or I will be as soon as I get my hands on a suitable weapon," she cooed up into his face with a honeyed threat.

If he didn't get her to see things his way, there was going to be hell to pay. Lying on her back as she was, Cassie's breasts were thrust up prominently by an abbreviated corset that had him gulping like a green gull. "Where did you get this?"

"Paris. Frenchmen love them; they're not as narrow-minded as thick-skulled Englishmen." Her taunt wasn't lost on him, but he'd learned a very hard lesson and learned it well. He suppressed his questions about how she'd know a Frenchman's preferences.

"Well unfortunately, you're married to an Englishman." Marcus fiddled with the several levers on the side of the sofa.

He'd spent many hours fantasizing what he'd do to her when he got her flat on her back on it.

A frown creased Cassie's brow at the sound of grinding gears. Her upper body rose, and her legs, forced to bend at the knees, were splayed by the folding bed, opening her to his avidly hungry eyes. His cock hardened even more. Its weighty fullness strained the buttons on his fly. Marcus grinned at Cassie's outraged scream.

She was as beautiful as he remembered. The damp pink flesh glistened between the plump folds. He reached forward reverently and brushed his knuckles over the unfurled bud at the apex of her cleft. Cassie's husky gasp was music to his ears.

"Don't," Cassie let out in a strangled whimper.

Marcus eyes widened. "You're sensitive to the lightest caress. I'd almost believe no one has touched you there these last three years. Is this true Cassie? Tell me." The beat of his heart increased. He brought his fingers to his nose and inhaled the heady muskiness.

"Go to hell. You don't deserve my fidelity, and as far as I'm concerned, you lost the right to question me." Her jaw jutted out mulishly.

Stubborn wench.

Marcus lifted the faux shaft and stifled a smile when he saw curiosity flare beneath the fury in her eyes. "I've perfected the mechanics." He wound the tiny knob and listened to the spring tightening. Rounded bumps rolled up and down the paper-thin, leather-sheathed shaft. "I attached one-sixteenth-inch diameter ball bearings to six chains and affixed them over a rigid hexagonal frame on the inside. Spring-loaded gears move them in a never-ending circle. I have a problem with the casing though. It has to be changed frequently; it stiffens and loses its suppleness when soaked."

"You should try a cover made from vulcanized rubber—" Cassie bit off her words, looking angry at herself for proffering the suggestion. But there was a softening in her demeanor, and he grasped it like a lifeline.

"Of course, the rubber would be waterproof and smooth to the touch. You've come up with the perfect solution. Until we've solved that thorny problem, I'd like your input on how this particular model works." He took a leap of faith and rolled the undulating object over her sensitive nipples. He watched them pebble through the lace. Her sensitivity was like an aphrodisiac and his breath hitched in his throat.

"I'm not one of your inventions, Marcus, to be fiddled with, until you get it right." She wasn't talking only about his creation. The low whirring filled the silence in the suddenly too hot room.

"You've always encouraged me in my endeavors, Cassie. Who better to evaluate my finest achievement in the manufacture of ladies comforters, but you, my, uh—muse?" He turned his head, kissed the side of her knee and watched the skin on her inner thigh ripple in response to his caress. She wasn't indifferent to him—encouraging.

Her lips twitched. "You'd be ruined if word got out that you even thought of making these."

"If I get to watch you dallying with it, I'd say it would be worth it." His gruff declaration brought a flush to her cheeks.

Cassie bit her lip and closed her eyes.

"Tell me you're not more than a little bit curious, Cass." He had to get one taste of her, in case she rejected him.

Marcus bent his head between her elevated legs and delicately speared his tongue into her cleft. Flattening his tongue, he swiped it up and down the damp flesh before curling it around her clitoris and then dipping into her core to lap at her nectar. Savoring what he'd been deprived of for so long, he nibbled on the pulsing tissues and swirled his tongue greedily in her dewy fluids.

She didn't give him an answer, but the change in the tempo of her breathing and slight upward shift in the angle of her hips told him what he needed to know. He had her tacit agreement.

There was nothing clinical about his actions when he brought the humming device down to press it against Cassie's pretty pussy. With it fitted lengthwise to her slit, the tiny balls rotated over her pearl and the nerve-filled folds of her labia.

If her tortured expression was anything to go by, he'd achieved his goal.

"For heaven's sake, put it in inside me!" It was a plea sheathed in a demand. Marcus happily complied and slowly eased it into her silken core. When only the dial at its base was visible, he pulled it back in small increments. He fucked her with long, slow strokes. Her soft mewls and his harsh breathing bounced off the walls.

"Tell me what it feels like, lovey," Marcus whispered, as he leaned forward and set his lips against her bared neck.

"Surely, you're joking," Cassie sputtered with a mixture of incredulity and disconcertment.

"I am not. Describe the sensations to me, please."

Cassie drew in a deep breath, licked her lips and let out a shuddery laugh. "Well, I feel incredibly full. The flesh within me is on fire, moving in a never-ending spasm around the dildo. The bumps on it soothe and stimulate all at once. I'm coming!"

Cassie's back arched off the button-studded sofa. She strained against her bonds and let out a strangled groan. After her drawn-out orgasm, she flopped back on the padding.

"Take it out, take it out. It's too much." She heaved up her hips. "I want *you* now."

Hearing her invitation, he all but ripped out the faux phallus. Fumbling with the bone buttons on his fly, he somehow managed to release himself. His cock bounded free like a thoroughbred springing through the gate.

He stepped between her thighs, but she was too low to sink into her comfortably. He pumped the lever to raise the platform and again stepped between her parted legs. The moment the crown of his cock made contact with her slit his balls tightened, and his hips bucked. Sliding the tip up and down her slit, he set the pin, gripped her hips and surged forward.

Heaven; it was pure heaven.

"Release my hands. I want to hold you." Heaving her hips up, she forced him deeper.

He didn't have to be asked twice. Marcus unbuckled the restraints, leaned in and captured her mouth for a long delayed kiss. She wrapped her arms around him with the same old fervency as she used to.

Cassie slipped her tongue into his mouth and flicked it back and forth in unison with his pumping hips.

Marcus felt Cassie groping around on the couch beside her body, and he pulled back, curious. She grinned wickedly up at him a second before the rolling balls crawled over the base of his organ. Ecstasy gripped him and a shudder wracked his frame.

From where he stood, he could see that she held the clock-work cock across her clit. Each time he eased out of her, his cock brushed against the implement.

Gripped by a dichotomy of sensations—the hot wet heat of her and the unrelenting movement of the beads rolling over his excited cock—Marcus released an animalistic howl. He lost all restraint and drove in and out of Cassie's welcoming channel with abandon, until he released his seed inside her.

"We must look like a sad pair, me trussed up like a capon

and you bare-arsed, with your trousers around your ankles." She laughed, cupped his face and kissed his lips.

Marcus eased out of her and wound the crank to lower her legs. He unstrapped her lower limbs and rubbed them.

"Will you come back to me?" He looked away, fearing a rejection.

"Well, now, that all depends," Cassie purred.

His head jerked up. "On what?" His heart pounded.

"On the other toys you plan to make." A sensual smile parted her lips.

Marcus grinned in response to her smirk. "Then you're back for good because I have an idea for a steam-powered..."

MUTINY ON THE
DANIKA BLUE

Poe Von Page

As far as uprisings go, the mutiny on the *Danika Blue* had to be the fastest on record. Before the captain could even complete his morning shite, drawn swords and weighty threats had subdued the commanding crew, forced the first officer down the refuse shaft and given way to a cacophony of brutish cries as the ship's appointed command stood down. Some credited the sheer number of mutineers and the swiftness with which they acted. Others blamed the sight of the captain's hands as they rose from the murky water bucket, trembling and ashen against the backdrop of deep space. If ever asked, though, Ailbhe would claim the mutiny was cinched upon sight of the nameless fellow who met the unfortunate and gruesome fate of explosive decompression, an effective act of persuasion, to be sure.

Ailbhe watched from her drawing table as Jael pushed past bemused crewmen toward the helm. His sky-blue coat brushed their knees as he moved and turning to address them, he gave each of his gloves a firm yank at the wrists. Full dress for a mutiny: only Jael would be so grandiose.

"Crewmen," he said, eyes scanning the deck for any signs of dissent, "I am the new and rightful captain of the *Danika Blue*. If you will not accept my authority it would be wise of you to step forward now. I have exhausted my cache of merciful acts and those who refuse to follow orders will be dealt with swiftly and without pity."

The deck creaked beneath the doddering feat of terrified men. Circling them all was Ziv, Jael's first in command and most trusted friend. Eyes narrowed and both daggers drawn, Ziv with his long black hair and sharp features looked like an animal on the prowl. He penetrated every gaze he could catch, professing without words his ferocious allegiance to Jael.

As Ziv circulated unspoken promises of reprisal, Ailbhe scanned the men trying to sense who among them might be inclined to skirmish with the ship's new regime. When she detected nothing she looked up at the captain to find him staring back at her, waiting for a signal. She nodded her approval and he let go a deep breath, placing his hands for the first time on the curves of the massive wooden helm of his new ship.

All fell silent as they watched the *Danika Blue* receive her new flag. As it was hoisted high over her creaking wooden body, a solar wind grabbed hold of it, revealing a single blue star over a background of black. A roiling wave of howls and whistles erupted from the crewmen as they acknowledged the *Danika Blue* now belonged to Captain Jael.

As the new captain conveyed his orders to Ziv, Ailbhe returned her attention to the vast space around them. She unfurled her sensors over the taffrail, past the barrier created by the atmosphere generator and deep into the cold black surrounding them. Quickly, her hands moved over the parchment laid out in front of her, dotting and smearing her coal as she mapped the spirit of the space they moved through. Her attention, projected far beyond the confines of the deck of the ship, was all the man behind her needed to begin skulking toward her.

The smell of whiskey on his breath, hot on the back of her neck, drew her back into herself. Before she could turn to face her attacker, the gleam of Jael's blade flashed centimeters from her face. As she shifted, slowly following the length of his steel, she caught a brief reflection of herself over the backdrop of space. She turned farther to see the blade pressing a sharp line into the aggressor's stubbly neck. A stream of sweat mixed with a thin line of blood pooled along its edge. Leering over him, ever present when Jael was in need was Ziv, daggers drawn once again.

"I...I was just going t-t-to ask the woman for some time, is all," he said.

Jael's steely eyes were fixed on him, unwavering. "With a knife?" He nodded to the small blade in the man's right hand.

"The c-c-captain is gone. What's it m-matter now?"

Jael's bottom lip pursed, dimpling his smooth chin. "*I* am your captain and *she* is mine. Befoul her again with so much as a glance and I will spill the contents of your belly onto the deck."

"We should toss her out with the trash, like we did the other. It's a slap to fate havin' a woman on board," rose another voice from deep within the gathering throng of men.

"Hear me now, all of you," Jael said stretching each syllable out. "The cartographer is mine. She is mine to observe, mine to command, and mine to...*spend time* with." An undertone of sneers and lurid remarks rose from the men. "If any of you think otherwise, or behave toward her in a manner unacceptable to me, your children's children will weep telling the tale of your slaughter."

Jael, with his sword still pressed against the man's neck, surveyed his crew. Most of them stood head down, their gaze averted from the captain's. The rest of them edged away from Ziv, as he looked at each of them as though he might devour them one by one. The only sounds were those made by the *Danika Blue* as her beams and planks creaked in time with the pulsing hum of the steam-driven atmosphere generator.

"Good," Jael said, withdrawing his sword and cleaning the filth left behind with a delicate handkerchief pulled from his breast pocket.

The men pottered back to their stations as the captain and Ziv bent their heads together for a hushed exchange. Ailbhe knew they were discussing her long before she saw Ziv's eyes dart in her direction. As Ziv strode back to the helm of the ship, Captain Jael turned his attention to Ailbhe. He slid his sword back into its ornate sheath and, maintaining his gaze, slowly bent at the waist. As he offered an angled arm, he said, "Ms. Ailbhe, join me in captain's quarters."

Ailbhe stared up at him, unmoving.

"Please," he said.

She dropped her coal on the drawing table and threaded her slender forearm inside the crook of his elbow. As they walked across the deck of the ship, she gazed at the contrast of the ebony lace of her gown against the pale blue of his wool coat.

He closed the door behind them and slid the wooden latch in place, securing it from outsiders. He had waited many long years for this room to be his and, in his mind, he had gone through these motions a thousand times before. Navigating his new quarters as though he had occupied the space since they left port two months ago, he quickly stowed his coat and poured her a glass of honeysuckle mead.

"Thank you," she said, wrapping her willowy fingers around

the glass and wetting her mouth with the sweet drink. As he
watched her, she licked her bottom lip and deftly flipped her
burgundy hair off her face. He loved her hair, the way it made
her look as though she were constantly in motion, like a shooting
star. He loved everything about her.

"Why do you wear nothing but black?" he said as he poured
himself a glass of the same.

"So the coal does not mark my clothes," she said without
inflection.

The left side of his mouth curled as he leaned against the
cherrywood desk behind him.

"I suppose you're wondering why I've called you to my quarters," he said as he set his drink down beside him.

"No."

"Surely you must be..."

"Do not presume to know my thoughts. You are naught but
an impudent worm that I should scrape from the bottom of my
boot."

Jael's shoulders broadened as his body tensed. "Yes," he said,
voice trembling with the effort of restraint.

"And as for your pathetic act of bravery on deck, do not
think for a moment that I was moved. You and I both know I
need no man to protect me."

Jael pulled at the thighs of his pants, trying to hide his
growing excitement. "Yes, I mean no. I was merely putting on
airs f—"

"Shut your maw, savage. Do you really think I care about
anything you have to say?"

He was thoroughly enamored with her beauty, even as he
was unnerved by the stare of her ecru eyes. "No," he said, barely
aware that his hands were steadily stroking his chest.

"I trust you still have the bung in your arse?"

Jael's eyes fluttered and abdomen twitched as his hind orifice clenched around the wooden stopper she placed inside him earlier that day. "Yes."

"It served its purpose then?" she said, the faintest hint of a smile creeping across her thin, peacock-colored lips.

"Every move I made, I thought of you. Every step I took, I felt you inside me. Directing me. Reminding me. Keeping me open, only for you."

"We shall see." With a brisk movement, she set her glass down and rose from her chair. As she stood, so did he.

"Take down your pants," she said.

He unlatched his belt and loosened his waistline, fumbling a bit with nervous anticipation. His pants dropped to the floor exposing him, naked from the waist down but for his shoes and socks.

"Turn around and place your elbows on the desk," she said as she moved towards him.

Stepping out of his pants with one foot, he kicked them aside with the other. He turned his back to her, bending at the waist and doing as he was told.

"Do not remove your forearms from the desk," she said.

"Yes, ma'am."

In one sharp movement she reached her hand round to the front of his face and placed the tips of two of her fingers over the openings of his nose. She yanked up and back, hard, bringing his face parallel to hers. "Have you forgotten, you half-witted ingrate, how to address your master?"

"No, sir. My apologies, sir."

"Pig," she said as she pulled her fingers back. She eyed them as contempt lined her forehead. "Disgusting. How dare you mark me with your filth? Clean them off," she said, holding them up to his mouth.

Not daring to pull his elbows from the desk, he craned his neck around to look her full in the eyes as he thoroughly cleaned her fingers. He licked and sucked them until she felt herself tighten beneath her skirt. She yanked them out of his mouth and brought her hand back only to land a firm slap across his face.

Spittle flew from his mouth, marking the map splayed out on the desk in front of him and his fingers crumpled the paper beneath them. Licking his stinging lip, he released a slow and tremulous breath.

She stepped back to survey him from behind, admiring the base of the wooden bung in his arse: lovely.

Reaching out and using the fingers of one hand, she spread his cheeks wide apart. With the two freshly cleaned fingers of the other hand, she pressed firmly on the plug, plunging it deeper inside him.

He gasped at the sensation and the hairs on his arms stood. A small groan escaped his mouth as he let his head fall forward.

Maintaining the pressure on the plug in his arse, she rolled her fingers in concentric circles, relentlessly mining inside him. She released his cheeks with her other hand and slipped it in front of him, cuffing his firmness and delighting in the sound it made as it rebounded against the desk.

She then grabbed on to his cock and pulled it forward, as she steadily and slowly drew the stopper from behind him. She felt his rear tighten and release as the widest part of it slid out of him, and she dropped it on the floor behind her.

She let go of him and he whimpered at the loss of her touch. "Please…" he said. "Sir, am I ready?"

"Do not be so eager, or you will wait another fortnight before I check again," she said knowing full well he could not see her unhooking her long black skirt from where it attached to her bodice. She had no intention of prolonging their play; his mutiny had brought that to an end. She needed to remind him of his place, prevent any urge to get uppity over his recent victory on ship. It had been a plan devised by her, after all.

Thick layers of black lace puddled around her feet as she adjusted the leather harness rounding her waist and thighs. She reached down to the pocket sewn onto the inside of her boot and slid out a glass shaft, which she quickly fastened into place at her Venus mound.

She took two steps toward Jael, regarding the dark hole of his arse and admiring the work the bung had done to open him over the past few days. She rubbed the head of her glass cock up and down the crack of his backside, intentionally avoiding the spot she knew he so longed for her to plumb.

Again, he whimpered and marveled at Ailbhe's ability to transmute torture into the sweetest nectar he could ever hope to taste. He longed for her to be inside him. He ached for her deep within his balls.

When he thought he could stand the teasing no longer, Ailbhe plunged deep inside him, burying her cock up to the harness and pressing her mound against his backside. The shock of it sent his arms straight out, flinging papers, a quill and a small bottle of ink off the desk and onto the floor. The clatter was loud and he was sure it would bring at least one of his men to the door.

"You like me inside you, don't you, worm?"

He struggled to pull his elbows beneath him. "Yes, sir," he breathed as she withdrew completely from him and pushed back inside him again.

He grunted and felt himself flush at the feminine tone of his cry.

"Ahhhhh," she said, "now you are learning. You just may please me yet." And with that, she began pumping in and out of his arse in time with the *Danika Blue*'s rhythmic hum. She went at it slow and steady, feeling each muscle twitch and every slight adjustment he made as he opened himself to her even further.

Approaching footsteps sounded from outside the locked door and soon after came knocking.

"Everything all right in there, captain?" Ziv's voice was unmistakable. Though he was Jael's closest confidant, even he did not know Ailbhe's true nature or that of Jael's relationship with her.

Without lifting his elbows from the desk, Jael twisted around to catch her in his periphery and raised his eyebrows in question.

"Answer him," she whispered.

"It's fine," he said, more breathy than he would have liked. "I'm fine, thank you," he repeated, this time more solidly.

She pulled back and quickened her pace, watching the buckles of her harness leave prints on the cheeks of his backside as they dug into his skin with each thrust. Again, an involuntary and undeniably femme grunt escaped from his mouth.

From the other side of the door, they could hear Ziv laughing and calling to inform the other crewmen that, "The captain's really givin' it to the mapmaker."

Ailbhe reached between his legs and clutched his balls, feeling them rock with every drive of her hips. His panting and grunting quickened. He could no longer hold himself up on his elbows, but yielded his chest to the desktop.

"Who is the captain of the *Danika Blue?*" she said.

"You are, sir," he said between frenetic gasps. "You are the captain. You are my captain. You are...captain...sir."

As the desk pitched along, millimeters at a time, Jael's glass of mead danced perilously close to the edge. She heard his stiff cock knocking on the desk as every plow pushed his chest farther across its surface.

Jael attempted to continue his line, the sentence he knew she wanted to hear, but overburdened with sensation, all he could manage to push from his lips was, "Sir...sir...sir..."

With every thrust, "Sir."

With every breath, "Sir," until she felt his body tense and his balls tighten and rise. She yanked down on them hard and pulled completely out of him, smacking his backside with an open palm hard enough to bring the blood to the surface.

Shocked, he looked back at her, knowing better than to say a word.

"You think you deserve to be brought before your captain?" she said.

"No, sir. No, sir, captain." He should have known better.

"On your knees," she said, pointing to the floor where he stood.

She walked around the desk, tracking spilled ink on the fallen maps until she was directly across from him. With a practiced flick of her fingers, she released her harness, laying it and her cock down.

He looked at it with deep longing in his eyes. "Later," she said.

With startling agility, she bounded up onto the desk and walked to the edge at which he knelt. He remained at her feet and traced the line of her black boots with his eyes until they ended just below her knees. Following up her leg, he noticed for the first time the faintest iridescent blue of her milky skin. Her bare sex crowned her legs and at the top of it all was her bodice, with all its hooks and cords. A shudder danced up his spine as he tried to take in the full sight of her.

She leaned her head forward, bringing her face into view, and looked down at him. Slowly, she squatted, opening her knees wide and spreading the folds of her sex in his face.

He could smell the scent of her, musky and intoxicatingly sweet. Without moving his head, he looked up into her eyes and awaited her next command.

"Worship," she said.

Jael's throat grabbed hold of his breath as he looked at the folds between her legs. He eyed the liquid glistening on the silken flesh of her valley, and thought to himself that he had never seen anything as beautiful as this. Of all the nebulae, glorious clusters of planets and radiant configurations of stars, this was the most magnificent thing he had ever gazed upon. It was as if he were staring into the eye of God Herself.

He hastily yanked off his gloves and tossed them over his shoulder. Raising tentative hands to stroke the velvety flesh of her inner thighs, he felt the contrast of their skin and cursed his hands for being rugged from a lifetime of work on ships. Pulling them back, he traced soft kisses down the inside of her legs, instead.

Over and over, he drew a line of kisses towards her sex and each time, he lingered there a bit longer. First, a nudge of his nose. Next, a kiss from his mouth. Then, a soft probe of his tongue. When he heard her purr softly in response, he reached both hands beneath the cheeks of her arse and held her up. In one fluid movement her legs swung over his shoulders as she leaned back, palms flat on the desk.

He dove into her, licking and sucking every fold and valley between her legs until he found the spot that made her tense and pant. He stayed there, quickening his pace and pressing her ever so slightly up and down with his arms.

With every movement of his tongue, he exalted her.

She sighed and moaned. He could feel the muscles in her arse and thighs flex and relax in his hands as she rocked her pelvis so that he no longer needed to hold her up.

His hands explored the rest of her, his fingers finding their way into both her openings as she continued to roll and grind against his face.

"I am your captain," she whispered, as she reached down with one hand and laced fingers through his silver hair. She pulled his face farther into her sex, smearing herself from his chin to his eyebrows.

He smiled despite himself, but did not stop tonguing, pushing his fingers deeper inside her and finding the corresponding spot within her that made her writhe. He worked his tongue and fingers in unison as she continued to whisper, "I am your captain. I am your captain."

Her words jumbled themselves and he felt her thighs begin to close around his head. He raised his elbows and forced her to stay open to him and with that last push she spasmed, clamping down on his fingers, letting her head roll back and thrusting her chest forward.

She screamed her release, shaking the bones of the *Danika Blue*. She bellowed her pleasure as an offering to the universe. She shook and twisted and yet he held her open, continuing his tongue and finger work until she brought her arms out from beneath her and melted onto the desk. Her body fell slack and he stayed there, between her legs, watching the rise and fall of her chest as her breathing slowed.

When it seemed as though she had drifted to sleep he rose from between her legs and walked around the desk. He viewed her from above, awed at the fierce beauty that shown through even her slumber. Gently, he slid one arm under her neck and the other beneath her knees and lifted her off the desk. With great reverence and care he maneuvered himself over to the bed, where he placed her amidst a pile of pillows. He drew a blanket of fur up over her body and sat next to her.

For a long while, he simply stared at her while she slept. At some point he rose to clean up the mess around the desk. When the room was fit, he arranged a blanket on the floor beside her and slept there.

In the morning, he awoke before she did and had hot tea and freshly baked muffins delivered. The smell of good things to eat roused her from her sleep and she ate what he offered her, without a word.

When they were both sated and washed, she turned to find him once again at the desk, his elbows on its surface and his arse open to her. She picked up the bung and gently inserted it in him, followed by a quick smack to his backside.

He took great care to dress her, clasping each strap, arranging each swath of fabric, and fastening each hook of her elaborate ensemble. He knelt before her and slid her glass cock back inside the pocket of her boot and stood back to admire her. When he was finished he dressed himself and they took a moment to regard themselves together in the mirror on the door: polarized twins, in every way.

As he placed his hand on the knob and moved to unlock the door, she spoke. "Perhaps tonight I may allow you to finish, but only if you perform well, first. You'll have to do better than you did last night."

He smiled and turned toward her. Without thinking, he kissed her on the mouth. It was the first time he had done such a thing and he quickly pulled himself back from her. She stood, smiling back at him, "Mutineer! You'll pay dearly for that tonight."

"I hope so, sir."

He swung the door open and she followed him out to the deck of the *Danika Blue*. As he assumed his place at the helm, and she hers at her drawing table, Ziv leaned in toward him.

"Captain?"

Jael stared at Ailbhe as she once again began mapping the energetic patterns around them that only she could sense.

"Captain?" Ziv repeated.

"Sorry, are you talking to me?" Jael said, unable to draw his eyes from Ailbhe.

"Yes, sir, captain. Whom else would I be talking to?"

"Right," he said and cleared his throat. "*I* am the captain. I am your captain, and she is mine."

DEVIANT DEVICES

Kannan Feng

The commander is a very busy man," the secretary said smoothly. "I'm sure you understand."

"Do you know," Victoria De Clemens said in wonder, gazing at the monstrosity, "I'm not sure I do?"

She guessed that it was a fainting couch, or at least, it had been at one point. It was long and low, with a stuffed roll of velvet at one end, but no other arms or sides. Between the rude struts of mechanical arms and leather straps, she could still see gilt legs and scrolled ornamentation. Despite the welcoming decadence of the purple velvet upholstery, there was a pervasive scent of machine oil that made her think of foundries.

"It's the commander's special design," said the secretary. He was a neat-looking, dark-haired young man with calm eyes behind square spectacles. He acted as if conversing with Commander Whitcomb's whores was an everyday task for him. Perhaps it was.

"Oh, I can see that it's special," Victoria said, well aware that she was stalling. "But what is it special *for?*"

The secretary's smile was patient and not unsympathetic.

"It is meant to prepare you," he said calmly. "Both fore and aft."

"Oh," she said. "I see."

For a girl who had been warming beds in a riverside brothel for months, an assignation with Commander Whitcomb could be the doorway into the easy life of a kept woman. It was a chance that she had fought for, and she was willing to do more to keep the position, but gazing at the half-decadent, half-industrial couch, she wondered how far she was really willing to go.

"Do I have to take off my clothes?" Victoria was pleased that her voice did not wobble. At twenty-two years old, and with a career that had spanned two continents, it took a great deal to surprise her, but the commander's couch was managing it.

"Down to the drawers and corset, yes. I'm staying to help you with the couch, but if you like, I'll turn my back."

"Do so," she said, regaining some of her haughtiness. "It's not like you're paying me."

He didn't peek as she removed her cream and scarlet morning gown. Next to the stark white of her camisole and knickers, her dark skin had a rich golden glow, and the whalebone corset gave her waist a sharp, vicious nip. In defiance, she left her black silk stockings and her polished boots on.

"All right then." This time she heard a distinct tremor in her voice and she squared her shoulders.

"Allow me to help you into position."

The secretary offered her a hand gloved in tight black leather. Surely those weren't military issue, she thought as he directed her toward the couch. The thing itself was surprisingly comfortable, a perfect place for a catnap if there weren't terrifying metal arms looming to either side, and a calm secretary removing his coat and opening a box of god knew what.

"What's your name?" she said suddenly. "I don't know what to call you."

He glanced up, a slight smile on his face. She realized that he was perhaps a few years younger than she herself was.

"You can call me Mercer," he said, "and if you don't want the commander to give us both hell, you'll let me get started."

She felt herself go hot and embarrassed at being caught out as afraid, but then he reached up to squeeze her hand.

"It's nothing to be afraid of," he said, so soft and quiet that she wasn't sure that he had spoken at all. Then he was standing up and away, arranging something on the nearby table.

"There are two wooden pegs to either side of the couch," he said. "Please place your legs to the outside of those pegs."

She found the worn wooden pegs and glanced over at Mercer. He had removed his jacket and now only wore his waistcoat and shirtsleeves, which were pushed to his elbows. He had not removed the black gloves and she realized that he was not going to.

It was very well for him to be calm, she thought angrily. He wasn't the one who was lying back on the bastard child of a foundry and a bordello.

When she let her legs fall to either side of the sturdy pegs, they were parted much farther apart than she thought they would be. It stopped short of straining her upper thighs, but her crotchless knickers fell open of their own accord. She knew that her curly black hair was being exposed to the room.

A little wider and anyone passing by could see the pink of her cunt, she thought, and she licked her lips. The exposure was frightening, but it was also arousing. She wanted someone to pass by and see how pink she was amidst all that dark curling hair.

Mercer glanced down at her, and despite his professional demeanor, she knew that he had taken a quick look. It made him more human, and she found a smile for him that made him swallow before he spoke.

"With your permission, Miss De Clemens, I need to prepare you for the machine."

"You do whatever you need to do, then," she said, feeling almost languid. The machine was new, but the way that he looked at her wasn't. It put her in control, and she watched him with curiosity as he stood between her widespread legs.

There was a high blush on his cheeks now, and she could see that his gloved fingers were covered with some sort of glossy oil. She knew what came next and she lifted her hips up to his fingers, sighing softly as they sunk in.

For all his youth, Mercer had obviously done this before, and he slicked her channel with quick, sure strokes. She could feel her own natural wetness rising to match, and she rocked up against his hand.

She was sure that he continued for a moment longer than he absolutely had to because he suddenly shook his head and withdrew his fingers. Her body arched after him for a moment, and then she forced herself to relax.

"That was pleasant," she commented, slightly breathless.

"I'm glad," he murmured. "I hope this part will be as well."

Her eyes widened as he held up a black rubber phallus. It had been expertly molded, and the blunt rear end was capped in steel threading. It looked large in his hands and she felt a momentary pang of apprehension and anticipation.

"What's the commander got that *that's* what I need to get ready for him?" she muttered, and Mercer only smiled slightly and shrugged.

The phallus was screwed into one of the jointed mechanical

arms and Mercer pivoted it around and bent it forward so that
it was pointed squarely between her legs.

Victoria couldn't take her eyes off it. It was a gorgeous toy,
but she couldn't ignore the metal arm behind it. It looked ready
to impale her, and she lifted her head to look at Mercer, who
was looking over the controls behind her head.

He caught her gaze and smiled reassuringly.

"This is going to make some noise," he warned her. "Be ready."
There was a series of clicks and then the machine began to whir.
It was not the loud, brutal clanking that she had been braced
for, and she was aware of a strong, steady vibration through the
frame of the couch.

She managed to observe all of that until she felt the head of
the phallus pushing at her cunt. It was gentle, just probing, but
she could feel the strength behind it. Victoria was beginning to
feel a panic rising in her throat, but then Mercer was kneeling
beside her, his gloved fingers spreading her open to allow the
phallus to enter.

"It's not perfect yet," he murmured. "I'm still needed for
some things."

"Well, thank god for that," she said, breathing hard. She
wrapped her arm around his shoulder, and having him there,
solid and human, helped as the phallus pushed into her body in
short, smooth movements.

Victoria took a deep breath and forced herself to relax. It was
large enough that it took time to enter her fully, but once it had,
it went perfectly still. She fell back against the couch, feeling
how stretched she was. Her hands were clenched into trembling
fists and she knew that her long black hair, so carefully pinned
up in the morning, was falling down in disarray.

"It'll be fine," Mercer was saying soothingly. "It'll be fine,
just relax."

She wanted to say something sharp to him, but his fingers were stroking the lips of her sex gently and soothingly, dancing close enough to her clit that she moaned.

"Are you read for more?" he asked, and she shook her head.

"Let me..." She gritted her teeth. "Let me see..."

He would have asked what she meant, but then she shifted her hips under his hand, withdrawing slightly from the mechanism before pushing herself back. It was large enough that she felt drawn taut, but she was slippery from the oil and Mercer's fingers. When she raised her hips a second time, the pressure turned into something much more pleasurable.

Victoria's sigh of relief turned into a surprised gasp when the phallus started to throb inside her. Somehow, it was swelling and trembling, and the ripple of sensations through her body made her moan.

Without noticing, she had squeezed herself against Mercer's chest. Her face was pressed against his shoulder, and when she addressed him, her voice was small and muffled.

"Did...did you do that?"

"I did." His voice was as hushed as hers and she knew that if she reached her hand into his neatly pressed trousers that she would find him hard and aching.

She wouldn't, though, and that thought delighted her too. He was the one ministering to her pleasure with this strange machine. It made him part of the machine and that excited her as well.

"More," she said imperiously, and that made him smile, even as he blushed.

He flipped another switch, and the vibration of the couch took a different timbre. After a barely perceptible shudder, the phallus withdrew from her almost completely before surging back inside. It was rigid in a way that a man wasn't, and the force behind it made her moan. It repeated the motion again and again, precise to the millimeter.

Victoria held herself perfectly still, but when the machine quickened its pace, she caught her breath and started to push her hips up against it. She couldn't help it. Even her fear of the strange device and her embarrassment about being exposed to the eyes of a man who was still entirely dressed conspired to excite her.

Somehow, her fingers were twisted into the sleeve of Mercer's shirt and his hand was between her legs again. He was less gentle this time, but his gloved fingers sought and found her clit with unerring accuracy. He stroked it firmly making her arch and thrash, and through it all, the phallus continued to pound into her relentlessly.

Victoria realized that she was about to climax just a moment before it happened, and then she shuddered, her body stiffening as if she had been shot through with electricity. She could hear her own moaning, high and breathless, and she clung to Mercer, burying her face in his shoulder and shaking so hard she was sure she would shatter.

Distantly, she heard him switch off the machine, and the phallus inside her came to a slow halt. When it was finally still, it rested halfway inside her. She was still wet, but tender too, and she started to slide back on the couch.

"Wait, allow me, please..." Mercer's voice was ragged but still polite, and one gentle hand on her shoulder convinced her to lie still if only to see what he would do next.

He flipped a few switches on the machine, and suddenly all of the tension from the mechanical arm was gone. The young secretary applied a fresh coating of oil to his fingers and gently slid them along the shaft of the phallus up to where it entered her now slightly swollen cunt.

Victoria sighed as his fingers moistened her cunt and the shaft of the phallus as well. When he removed the phallus from her body, there was no swift pain, only a long, smooth slide that ended with a gentle moan escaping her lips.

"You're beautiful," he said softly, laying the phallus somewhere that she couldn't see.

"Thank you," she muttered, pressing her legs closed. The machine had left a lingering soreness that blurred the line between a sensual memory and a physical pain.

"We're not done yet," he said as she stretched.

She glanced at him, feeling languorous but playful.

"You're pleased that we're not done yet," she said teasingly, and he smiled with one corner of his mouth.

"I am always pleased to spend time ministering to a lady as lovely as you."

She laughed at his gallantry, but then he glanced behind his shoulder and became all business again.

"Will you get up on your hands and knees, please?" he asked.

"Ah, yes," she commented. "Mustn't be lazy, now."

She unwound her legs from the wooden pegs and assumed the position that he indicated. The cushioning of the fainting couch was firm and now thoroughly stained with her wetness. The scent excited her further and she smiled, catlike, at Mercer.

"It must be nice," she said, "getting to play with the commander's bits of pretty."

"A gentleman ought not talk about those things." He said it with such primness that she broke into laughter.

"And what a gentleman you are, with such a thing in your hands!"

Mercer was holding a smaller phallus now. It was slender and only as long as her own small hand, but otherwise it was identical to the first. He fixed it to a second mechanical arm.

"I'm not a gentleman," he admitted, "but I do try to do my best."

He pulled the opening in the crotch of her drawers wider. He was polite, but she knew that he was looking, too, and that pleased her more than it should have.

She braced herself on all fours as his gloved fingers pushed at her rear hole. He had used oil and he had even warmed it in his hands, but she flinched as he eased one finger inside.

"Have a care," she said, breathing deeply.

He murmured an apology, but he continued, drawing his finger in and out until she was softened enough that he could add another. She shifted her weight on the couch, easing back against him and forcing herself to relax.

Mercer was so slow and gentle that she felt her eyes drifting closed as she was rocked back and forth by the motion of his hand. Almost without noticing it, she fell forward on her elbows and arched her back. It put her ass up even higher and Mercer made a sound that was halfway between a sigh and a moan.

"So beautiful," he said quietly, and she wanted to ask if he said that to all the commander's whores.

He withdrew his fingers, and for a moment, she felt empty. Then she felt the oiled head of the second phallus pushing against her opening and Victoria wondered if it wasn't too much after all.

"It feels larger than it looks," she said, grunting as it started to push in.

"Yes," he said agreeably. "That's usually the way of it."

The thought of the polite young secretary with his pants down around his ankles and his ass high in the air caused a rush of heat to come to her cheeks. The leather phallus was moving more slowly than the first one had, and even as she felt herself open to it, she glanced back at Mercer.

"Oh, aye?" she said softly. "Do you know, then?"

The change on his face was gorgeous. His lips parted and the color came up to his cheeks. It was all the answer that she needed, but he nodded.

Victoria smiled, rocking her hips gently. The head of the phallus popped past the tight ring of muscle and she groaned. His hands were parting the cheeks of her ass so that the mechanism could enter her more smoothly, but she reached back and grabbed his sleeve.

"Have you been where I am?" she asked huskily. "Bent over with a machine fucking you the way a man would?"

He licked his lips (oh, that lovely pink tongue, what she could do with *that!*) and he nodded again.

"The commander...the commander has varied tastes."

"No wonder you're so good with this—ahhh!"

The phallus entered her to the hilt. It was sunk deep, and her fingernails dug into the velvet cushions. It wasn't wide, but it was long, and she had to fight the urge to pull away.

"Shh, shh, there, it's all in," he said, stroking her hair. He was still making fine adjustments to the machine, and it withdrew slightly. She squirmed, but Mercer put a gentle hand on her waist, keeping her still.

"Did you like it?" she asked in a conspiratorial whisper.

"I screamed the house down," he whispered back. "Yes."

The machine whirred to life and she felt the vibrations of the pistons built into the chair just a second before the phallus started thrusting into her.

These strokes were long and smooth, with none of the increasingly quick movements that she had experienced before. It really was getting her ready, she thought. When a man came to fuck her, he would find her well prepared. She wondered what it was like to fuck someone who had been opened so precisely.

Victoria glanced at Mercer, who was watching the machine intently, and suddenly, she longed to see him bent over and taking a good fucking. She wanted to see that polite mouth open in a scream of pleasure and she wanted to see him bury his face in the cushions and submit to it no matter how embarrassed he was.

"You're smiling," he said quietly, and she laughed. Or at least, she started to, but it came out a moan instead. The machine's tempo hadn't changed, but she was rocking back on it. It was extraordinary to fall back on the thrust and fullness of the machine without feeling a man's hands on her hips and his balls bouncing against her ass, and she groaned in surprise at the pleasure it brought her.

She knew she could depend on the steadiness of the rhythm, and she balanced her weight on one elbow, reaching between her thighs with her free hand. Victoria knew that Mercer saw what she was doing, because he drew breath suddenly and sharply. He couldn't have seen much, with her drawers in the way, but he had to know what her hand disappearing between her legs meant.

Victoria focused on how full she felt as she played with her clit. It was sore, but deliciously so, and she thought about the machine, built for the enjoyment of a man she hadn't even met yet, but built for her enjoyment too; oh, yes, because she was quickly falling in love with it.

Soon she was plunging two fingers in and out of her wet cunt, loving the ache of being so well used. Her mind was full with the hum of the machine, and the way the vibrations traveled throughout her whole body.

She suddenly thought of both of the pistoning arms arranged to fill her in both holes at once and she shrieked as she came, convulsing around her fingers and around the phallus that was still moving in and out of her with the beat of a dedicated military drummer.

Her own cries echoed in her ears and it felt like the bones in her body would no longer support her. Distantly, she was aware of the machine slowing and then stopping as Mercer flipped a few switches.

Victoria whimpered when it pulled out of her completely, and then she curled over on her side, watching as Mercer tended to the machine.

"When will the commander be seeing me?" she asked lazily. She had almost forgotten she was here for a job.

"He won't be," Mercer said, folding the mechanical arms away. "Or, well, he already has."

Victoria sat up, ignoring a twinge in her nethers.

"What are you talking about?" she demanded, but she thought she might already know.

"As I mentioned before," Mercer said, a rueful smile tugging at his lips, "the commander is a man of diverse tastes."

"He's been watching."

"Yes. It's what he does. Don't worry, you'll certainly get paid."

Victoria bit her lip. As diverting as the machine had been, it wasn't the kept position that she was looking for.

Mercer looked up at her. He had rolled up his sleeves to deal with the machinery, but the gloves, glossy with lubricant and smelling of her, were still on his hands.

"If I know anything about the commander's tastes, and I think I do," he murmured, "I think he's quite enjoyed himself, and that he will be requesting you in the future."

"Well, I certainly hope so," she said. "Anything you think I could do to sweeten my chances?"

Mercer's quick glance at the machine told her that there

certainly was, and she smiled. A few moments before, she thought that she was done for at least an hour, and now she was looking at some of the other arms of the fainting couch speculatively.

"Tell me which one is your favorite," she said, "and we'll go from there."

THE
PERFECT GIRL

Jay Lawrence

"We call her Crepe de Chine. There's no point speaking to her. She doesn't understand English."

"Perfect. I find it spoils things when they talk."

"As you wish, sir."

I crouched on the vast mahogany bed on all fours like a dog. Warm air caressed my naked buttocks. My drawers were lowered, skirt and petticoat raised. The madam retreated, pausing in the doorway to swiftly count the price of my humiliation, then the door closed with a soft click. We were alone, my Mr. Friday Night, his veiled lady friend and me.

"Are you obedient, I wonder, Crepe de Chine."

The man voiced his question as a statement. In fact, I understood English perfectly well, having come from Peckham not Paris, but Mrs. James liked her girls exotic and mute. I bowed my head, auburn curls cascading over white shoulders. The man removed his jacket and took a turnip watch from his waistcoat pocket. Outside, a locomotive thundered past and I wondered if he was a railway enthusiast. The tall, slightly gimcrack house trembled and the solid bed vibrated in sympathy. A cloud of soot and steam stained the bedroom window. My nipples pressed against the stringent embrace of my chemise, stays laced extra-tight, hard enough to make my breathing fast and light as I panted in the heat of the blazing fire in the grate. I was indeed obedient. It paid very well.

"Touch the girl's bottom."

Mr. Friday gestured and his companion took a dainty, rather stiff step forward. It wasn't very unusual for a gent to bring another girl along but usually it was another slut, a popular male fantasy being watch-two-girls-at-play or sometimes watch-my-slut-being-whipped-by-another-whore. I didn't mind. I liked the satiny, cushiony feel of another naked girl. I liked their smell of musk and sweet scent and sweat. Gloved hands patted and appraised my rear. I arched my spine and moaned quietly, theatrically. The girl's touch felt a little awkward, inexperienced but keen. Pat. Pat. Pat.

"*Explore*, Victoria. Find the wet place between the girl's legs."

I helpfully raised my behind and parted my thighs, anticipating the feel of buttery suede against my rapidly moistening quim. Sometimes clients get you going, often they don't. This man and his rather well-behaved girl did. Surprisingly strong fingers stroked my wet cleft. I closed my eyes and ground my hips, using the girl like a toy, pleasuring myself. Suddenly, she slid two fingers deep inside me and I yelped, more from surprise than discomfort. She smelled a little odd. What was it? Moth-balls. I opened my eyes and stole a glance at her. Good heavens, she had to be over six feet tall! She was rather angular, dressed in schoolmistressy navy blue, her black glossy hair swept back in ravenlike wings beneath a small veiled hat. I could not see her face for the heavy lace, just a hint of strong cheekbones and a wide voluptuous mouth. The jacket of her costume was primly buttoned right up to her chin.

"Good, Victoria."

Mr. Friday sounded as if he was praising a small child for learning to tie her bootlaces. Victoria nodded almost imperceptibly then abruptly withdrew her fingers, sliding them out of my willing pussy with a satisfying plop. I pouted and wriggled so that my nipples pushed against the lacy trim of my chemise, creamy, full breasts threatening to spill. I thought about being spanked, not too hard, enough to turn my buttocks a lovely shade of rose like a cherub's blush. Mr. Friday seemed to be consulting his pocket watch again. Perhaps he was one of those academic types—was I an experiment? Maybe the rather haughty girl in attendance was his laboratory assistant, ready to take down my particulars, each gasp and moan elicited by her long, firm fingers recorded in a special book.

"Touch the girl's breasts, Victoria."

The smell of camphor grew stronger. Poor girl—did the professor pay her so shabbily that she had to resort to secondhand clothes? She smelled like an old lady on a rare Sunday outing. I sat back and let her explore my ample bosom. Slowly, she undid the ribbons of my chemise and lifted the mounds of flesh free, holding them first with one hand, then with both hands, as if gauging their size and weight. I wondered if her old man had a portable set of scales with him. I could tell them the size all right. They were like melons. My nipples looked full, puffy and pink in the reddish light from the leaping flames. I wondered if Mr. Friday's cock was hard and whether it strained against the front of his trousers, but I didn't dare look. Miss Prim's hands massaged my breasts, and I now moaned quite genuinely, no theatricals required. The girl had strong hands. I noticed how big they were, almost like a man's but more delicately shaped.

"Good, Victoria," repeated Mr. Friday. Victoria's hands left my quivering, aching tits and I felt like crying. My thighs were wet, sweet musky juice dribbling from the source of my pleasure. I wondered if Victoria could wield a bamboo cane, imagined her stern, governessy figure switching a delicate pattern of scarlet welts onto my helpless behind.

"Now step back."

The room was very quiet and rapidly becoming stiflingly hot. Victoria withdrew, stumbling slightly on the fringe of the thick Turkey rug. Mr. Friday caught her arm to steady her and again she nodded, a small, curt inclination of her head. I wondered what was next as he referred to his watch again. My breasts and pussy throbbed, fully aroused but painfully neglected. I needed release. Perhaps he was observing the effects of intense stimulus followed by deprivation on the common or garden bordello slut. I tossed my curls and moved my hands toward my quim. I could smell myself, an intoxicating mix of strong musk and lily of the valley scent. It wouldn't take much to send me over the edge of pleasure.... I thought of the wide voluptuous mouth behind the modesty veil. I imagined full moist lips against my fat shiny bud, teasing, kissing, licking, sucking, bringing me to the climax of my twenty years. But no.

Sir and madam retreated to a corner of the red room, which resembled a velvety cell with its heavy brocade drapes, thick rugs and steadily blazing coals. I knew Mr. Friday would get annoyed if I frigged my nubbin, so I hung my head and let my curls swing in wanton abandon, a harlot, a hussy, a slut fit for spanking. It didn't work. Mr. Friday rummaged in a carpetbag.

What was inside? A set of brass calipers to measure the width of my neglected arse? I watched him quizzically as he finally retrieved a large ball of string. Oh, lord! Did my roses need support? Sighing, I resumed my animal stance, ensuring my tits and bum were more on show than ever. If I'd had a sign reading TITS AND ARSE—PLEASE HELP YOURSELF, I'd have hung it over the bed.

Mr. Friday advanced with the string and began to wrap it round my wrists. Hmm, usually gents who liked that trick would do it with a length of cord or fine silk, not common garden twine. I hoped it wouldn't slice into my skin. I had to work as a pretty thing, not a badly wrapped parcel.

The girl held back, silently observing her professor as he stooped and wrapped, tied and retied and generally turned me into a game of cat's cradle. When he had finished, I didn't know whether to laugh or cry. I had had some odd things done to me since joining Mrs. James's establishment, but this took the biscuit.

Another train passed and, again, the building shook to its crumbly foundations. My feeble bonds seemed to sing in response. I discovered that, flimsy as the string appeared, any attempt to move was rewarded with a sharp stab of pain. Hmm, I hadn't taken Mr. Friday for a sadistic sort. I frowned in his direction, but he didn't appear to notice. My eyes grew wide as he delved in his portmanteau and proudly retrieved a large oak paddle. Ouch! So, I was to have my poor unprotected arse slapped crimson with a polished implement straight from a home for wicked girls, was I?

Involuntarily, I clenched my buttocks tight and waited for prof to give Victoria the nod. I thought of her strong, almost manly grip. I wondered if her wrist matched her hand—powerful, measured strength. It would be a long, tear-inducing paddling of my humble rear... Mr. Friday's voice changed.

"Victoria—bend over."

Was I hearing things? So, I wasn't to be the whipping girl? I watched with an odd mixture of relief and annoyance as my client guided his silent girl to the ottoman at the foot of the bed. Meekly she knelt on it, having flipped her skirt and petticoat up to reveal prim starched drawers. Her bottom looked firm and taut beneath the plain white linen. A paddling would surely leave painful welts on such a trim, lightly padded behind. I began to feel sorry for the girl and hoped she was being well rewarded for her trouble. Or maybe she was madly in love with her tormentor, eccentric as he seemed. I waited for him to unfasten and drop her drawers but he didn't. Ha! So she wasn't to take it on the bare. Was that for reasons of modesty or to avoid leaving marks that someone else might see?

I almost felt superior, my own bottom royally bared and bosoms on full display. I crouched, fully trussed, waiting with bated breath for the first stroke to fall. Mr. Friday carefully removed his cufflinks and rolled up his sleeves. The action excited me, sent a stirring rush of fresh blood to my quim. He was stronger than he looked. I watched the sinews on his forearms as he flexed and made a few practice swings with the paddle. It resembled a small cricket bat. Miss Prim didn't bat an eyelid beneath her lacy veil. I gave her that—she was a plucky one all right.

Mr. Friday moved to the foot of the bed. I could sense his excitement—he had left the starchy rigmarole of bossing Victoria behind and was ready for the main event of tanning her naughty little arse. I held my breath and realized that my heart was beating strong and fast. He raised the paddle and smartly brought it down against the back of Miss Haughty's thighs with a satisfying *thwack*.

I braced for a howl but the room remained quiet. The only sound was the crackling and hissing of the fire in the grate. *Thwack*. She still maintained a stoic silence, and they were not gentle strokes. I found that each time he raised the paddle *I* braced myself and the string tightened about me like a twiney web. I winced yet could not help myself. I wanted her paddling for myself. *Thwack, thwack, thwack.* I jolted rhythmically with each sharp retort against the girl's well-starched, no doubt throbbing behind. How could she bear it? I began to be mesmerized, trapped in the steady rhythm of wood meeting linen-clothed skin, imagining the fiery heat beneath, the burning, the terrible flaming pain. On and on, *thwack* and jolt, my Lilliputian bonds tightening and relaxing, rhythmically squeezing my helpless tender flesh. I was a fly trapped in a spider's web. *Thwack,* silence, fire, jolt, squeeze. Heat, flesh, bonds, wood, soft sweet skin. Helpless, I realized I was reaching a monstrous climax. He hadn't touched me. She hadn't touched me. My eyes were transfixed on the final savage smack of oak on firm, unbending flesh. I cried out, cunt on fire, body crisscrossed with a maze of scarlet tracks. He had whipped his girl and I had scored my own flesh in my jolting, unrequited lust.

I collapsed on the counterpane, gasping like a fish out of water. Mr. Friday was rolling down his sleeves, helping the silent girl to her feet, straightening her clothes. I wondered if she'd be able to walk or if they'd have to fetch a hansom cab and make her sit on a cushion all the way home.

"That all went rather well, didn't it?" said Mr. Friday.

Victoria stood by the door, as expressionless as ever. I wondered if she were a bit simple and whether Mr. Friday was a cad, taking advantage of a poor defenseless idiot girl. But surely she would have shrieked and shrieked...

The spell of domination was wearing off, like the morning after a champagne debauch. I looked down at myself. My poor body was a right old mess, clearly marked by the string, and I looked as if I'd been captured and tortured by Her Majesty's Royal Mail. Suddenly, I was furious and found my tongue.

"Just look at me!"

Mr. Friday jumped as if he'd been shot.

"I thought you didn't speak English." He looked as if he had a bad smell right under his nose.

"I'll want paid extra for *this*, I can tell you!" I squawked, twisting to examine my striped legs.

Mr. Friday sighed and addressed the china dogs on the mantelpiece.

"Why must they always open their mouths? It does so ruin everything when they talk."

"There's nothing wrong with the way I speak." I bristled with indignation. Talking back to a gent was likely to get me fired, but I'd had about enough of the high jinks and kinks at Mrs. James's bordello. My skin was a mess and I felt like knocking Mr. Friday's smug block off.

"Nuffink wrong with the way aee speak?"

He was mocking me, making fun of my Peckham accent. Could I help that I wasn't from a well-to-do home? Would I be lying there all trussed up like a prize Christmas turkey if I was? With one monumental, painful effort I freed my wrists and picked up a pillow and aimed it at the professor's sanctimonious head. He promptly ducked and it hit Miss Iron Derriere squarely in the face. Oops. She staggered back and let out a vicious hiss. I thought she called me a bad name and I picked up another feathery missile. The second pillow flew through the air with twice the force of the first. To my horror, the girl's head twisted sharply to one side with a loud crack. I had broken her neck. It would be the gallows for me. Then—good lord—*steam* began to issue from the neck of her costume. She slowly slid to the floor, legs sticking out before her, like a collapsed marionette. I watched in horrified fascination then jumped as there was a loud bang and her head flew off! A quantity of small brass objects like the mechanism of a clock clattered to the floor. Cogs, springs and levers scattered to the corners of the room. The headless girl twitched violently like the monster from Miss Shelley's lurid tale.

"What is going on?"

An outraged Mrs. James threw open the door, all baleful glare and crackling bombazine. Victoria let out another terrible hiss, shook in a final mechanical spasm then was still.

"Professor Higgins, I really must insist that you make less noise! My other gentlemen…"

Mr. Friday crouched on the rug beside the broken clockwork girl. I stalked past him and out of the room as he continued to mutter to himself.

"She was the perfect girl. They always spoil *everything* when they talk…."

Then I realized I had seen his face in the newspapers. He was that geezer who lured a poor defenseless flower seller from her pitch at Covent Garden and tried to turn her into a duchess. Mad as a hatter.

DR. MULLALEY'S CURE

Delilah Devlin

'd been warned that the doctor was a bit eccentric; that he
dabbled in machinery and had been ostracized by others in
his profession for the lengths he went to please his patients.

"You'll never find another employer," I was told. "Not
once they see your only reference is Doctor Mullaley." The
mad Irishman. The charlatan who promised cures to bored
housewives and whose waiting room hadn't been empty since I
arrived for my first day's work. If I hadn't already been turned
away at every other respectable physician's practice, I might
have heeded the advice. However, those warnings only served
to stir my interest.

I was intensely curious about the nature of the doctor's cures
and even more so about the conditions he treated, but they were
only spoken of in whispers and never in the presence of an unmarried woman. This made me wonder why he'd hired me, not that I
complained. One glance at his tall rangy frame, frosty blue eyes
and dark, slicked-back hair, and my misgivings evaporated.

However, my curiosity about the man and his practice wasn't to be satisfied at that moment because the doctor waved me toward the reception desk where I worked at fitting in patients who walked in without an appointment, a task I found akin to cinching in the waist of a corset. There was only so much ribbon one could pull before something gave.

That something was the inimitable Mrs. Davies. She arrived in a dudgeon, cheeks flushed, eyes a little wild. It was a very balmy afternoon, and the painstaking curls at the sides of her cheeks had wilted and were stretching toward her jaw like earthworms. I couldn't help staring while she tapped the counter with her finger insisting her needs were of the highest import. If she didn't receive a treatment that afternoon, *somebody* would hear about it.

At wit's end, I gave her a false smile, said I'd find the doctor and escaped down the corridor to the treatment rooms.

The corridor was as handsomely appointed as the waiting room with rich oak paneling below the rail, and burgundy brocade above it. But gaslight sconces were placed so far apart that shadows loomed between the doorways.

I paused at the first room to listen, hoping to hear the low timbre of the doctor's voice. Faint moans came through the door, but since they didn't have an urgent edge, I hurried to the next and pressed my ear against the wood.

Hands curved over my shoulder. "Pardon me, Nurse Percy." The doctor firmly pushed me to the side and strode into the room.

Glancing around his tall frame, I spotted Mrs. Headley, who lay on a table that tilted with the lower half split in two.

My jaw sagged as I noted that while she was clothed in a sacklike gown, Mrs. Headley lay bared from the waist down, her legs strapped to the split "legs" of the table. Her fingers dug into padded handles at the sides. Most curious, there was a long, slender trough running from a tank latched to the ceiling, very like a toilet's reservoir. The trough emptied into a funnel, which ran into a tube. The tube passed through a device with turning wheels that clicked like a clock's inner gears and then ended at a nozzle that spurted water in rhythmic pulses toward the juncture of Mrs. Headley's thighs.

How odd, I thought.

Mrs. Headley moaned. Her gaze roved restlessly until she lighted on the doctor. "Please, Raymond, I can't take much more. I'm very sure I'm ready for the next stage of my treatment."

The doctor stood between me and Mrs. Headley so I couldn't see what he did, but then he aimed a frown over his shoulder. When he turned back, I entered the room and shut the door behind me, staying quiet as a mouse. He turned off the nozzle. The rhythmic splashes stopped, but wet slurping sounds filled the silence.

"I feel...nearly...oh, the agony...oh, doctor!" Mrs. Headley gave a choked little scream, her upper body arching on the table before settling again. Her flushed cheeks shone with sweat, but the smile she gave the doctor was so filled with gratitude I felt a stirring of something akin to pride for the doctor's skill.

However, pride wasn't what tightened the feminine parts of me. Somehow, just knowing where the doctor's hands were made the room feel quite warm.

Doctor Mullaley pulled down his patient's gown, patted her hand and turned, drawing up short when he spotted me standing in front of the door. He jerked his chin to indicate I should precede him.

Feeling nervous and a little embarrassed by what I'd witnessed, I stepped into the hall and wrung my hands. "I wouldn't have interrupted, doctor," I blurted, "but there's a woman at the reception desk demanding an appointment. Frankly, I thought she'd push right past me to find you if I hadn't said I would go."

"Let me guess, Mrs. Davies?"

I nodded.

He sighed and looked up and down the hallway. "I have another hydropathy machine in the treatment room at the end of the hallway. While you were spying, did you happen to notice what I did to turn it off?"

"The hose from the reservoir? Yes."

"The reverse turns it on. Take Mrs. Davies there. Find her a gown and help her out of her clothes. Start the machine. I'll be along when the others have finished their treatments." He gave me a narrowed glance that seemed to note my appearance for the first time. "After you've settled her, find me. I think you might work out after all."

I nodded, blushing beneath his approval, and walked on air back to the reception room. Even Mrs. Davies's rude behavior as she complained all the way down the hallway couldn't dampen my mood. She didn't relent while I undressed her until it came to her corset. Claiming I'd scratched her, she slapped my hands away, saying she'd manage the garment on her own. Not that she really needed one; any garment constructed to shape her enormous belly would have required true engineering genius.

When it came to setting up the hydropathy machine, Mrs. Davies showed me exactly where the nozzle needed to be placed for "maximum efficacy." That lesson left me blushing because I set the nozzle to squirt at the knot at the top of her sex.

With Mrs. Davies quiet at last, I went in search of the doctor.

I followed the sound of grinding gears and whistling pistons to another treatment room. Inside, the patient lay with her gown scrunched around her middle. Clamps with wire tethers were attached to her nipples. Her legs were spread and elevated, and another device pressed against her sex.

The doctor glanced up as I entered. "There you are. See the lever on the side of the machine?" He pointed to a large tin box with dials and gauges on the front and from whence the devices at the woman's nipples and sex were connected.

I nodded, spying the lever at the side.

"Throw it up to start the current."

The moment I did, a curious humming sounded from between the patient's legs. Her eyes squeezed shut, and she moaned around the gag tied behind her head.

I glanced at the doctor, a question in my eyes.

He bent toward my ear. "She thinks it's sinful to make noises when she culminates."

"Culiminates?"

The corners of his shocking blue eyes crinkled. "Nurse Percy, has the mister never *culminated* when in the throes of his husbandly duties?"

My mouth dropped. "I've never married or witnessed a man's...*culmination*. Are you telling me a woman can too?"

His gaze honed on my expression. "For the sake of your apprenticeship, I think it will be my duty to demonstrate my cures."

My heart skipped a beat. "Just what sort of conditions are you treating, sir?"

The doctor checked the gauges, gave the woman a pat on her hand, then waved me toward the door. "Step outside."

In the hallway, he stood close with his hands held behind him. Mine, I clutched against my belly as I listened to him describe the many illnesses of the body and mind that occurred when a woman didn't release the noxious poisons boiling inside her. If a husband wasn't willing or able to assist, then a woman sought the help of a doctor who specialized in such things.

"And these machines...?"

He brought his hands forward, and I noted the length and thickness of those digits. "The machines save my hands from aching after endless pelvic massages."

That was a term I had heard before. I'd even attempted to perform it on myself a time or two, but I'd given up frustrated just before I'd discovered the mystery that lay at the end of the quest.

"Doctor, I am unmarried but hope to be some day. I cannot allow you to directly...massage...that region," I hissed.

His lips twitched. "Which is not a problem, dear nurse. I have designed devices meant to assure a woman's sensibilities aren't violated. Stay after work, and I will demonstrate them all."

The rest of the day passed in a blur as I learned to apply the devices to other women's tender breasts and nether regions, all the while admitting a deepening sensitivity in my own body.

When at last the office closed, the doctor led me into the treatment room that held the widest array of machinery, including one device still covered in a tarp in a corner. My glance must have lingered there.

"Something I'm developing," he murmured, "but I'm looking for a volunteer to test it."

When I opened my mouth, he shook his head. "You're unmarried. This machine would shred your maidenhead."

After all I'd witnessed this day, I thought there wasn't a blush left in me, but my face heated.

His fingers trailed my cheek. "There's a gown on the table

that I'd like you to wear. When you're ready, just open the door." With that, he left.

The gown was a thin, dove-gray silk. I passed my hand beneath it and realized my whole body would be visible. Still, I didn't hesitate to remove my clothing. He was a physician after all. I would do this in the name of my education and the furtherance of science.

When I was dressed in nothing but the gown, I opened the door a crack and peeked into the hallway. He stood with his back to the door. I cleared my throat, and he turned to meet my one-eyed glance. "I'm sure you're lovely in that gown, but I promise not to ravage you," he said, his voice a lovely rumble. "Open the door, Nurse Percy."

Taking a deep breath, I stood to the side and let him enter then locked the door behind him even though I knew there wasn't anyone else about.

"Lie on the table, please."

His brusque voice, the professional one devoid of amusement, was back. This was the voice that reassured the most skittish of his patients. His actions were just as clinical and brusque as he ran straps around my thighs and set my hands on cushioned squabs with a warning to keep them there.

As docile a lamb as any of his patients, I let out a quiet gasp when he pulled up the gown, showing care as he freed it from the straps before smoothing it up my thighs to bunch at my hips. I managed to remain silent when he parted the table's divide and thus my thighs, even though he came to stand between them and fingered the dark hair that cloaked my Venus mound.

"I thought it would be coarse," he said, "as curly as your hair is."

My blush deepened, but I didn't attempt a retort as he didn't seem to require one. He parted my folds and swirled his fingers around the opening. "To stimulate you, my dear. I want your pretty little nubbin to come out and play."

"But you didn't do this before you started the machines for Mrs. Davies or Mrs. Smith."

"Before I designed my devices, all my treatments began with direct stimulation," he said, sliding his fingers between my folds to capture the moisture then smooth it around and around. "But my hands tired, and I could only handle so many patients a day. The demand grew, and I knew I had to do something or see them find physicians who might have less care for their sensibilities."

"Your machines provide a service, I know. I've seen the transformations. Even Mrs. Davies left cooing like a dove."

He flashed me a grin, and then his gaze dropped between my legs again. "There she is. A little shy this one, but a lovely dark pink. Have you ever seen your love knot?"

"That's what it's called?" I said, jerking when his thumb rubbed it.

"It's called many unsavory things and a couple of medical terms that aren't flattering at all, but for you Nurse Percy, it's a love knot. You're very sensitive. I'll be sure to adjust the nozzle burst to something softer than I would for a woman who has had hers tweaked by a lover a time or two."

"You really shouldn't say such things to me."

His eyes narrowed as he studied my face. "Nurse Percy, I'm your employer, and my business is one that requires civility and discretion when dealing with patients. However, you will need to accustom yourself to frank terminology. You will hear it now and again from some of the ladies' own mouths. They cannot help themselves when they are...culminating."

I swallowed hard, still so aware of where his fingers trailed and of the fact that liquid flowed from inside my body, which he used to swirl over my folds and that sensitive, swelling nubbin he seemed to be fascinated with.

Something like a cramp tightened my belly and my hips curved. "Doctor?"

"Yes, dear. Let's begin."

He brought the hose down over his shoulder and took a seat on a stool, which placed his face very near the juncture of my thighs. While my eyes widened in shock, that maddening tension began to curl around my womb. Not an unpleasant sensation, but breathtaking nonetheless.

He'd removed his jacket, his shirt and undershirt. With his broad, lightly furred chest bare, he met my questioning gaze. "The water will splash. And I wish to be close enough to gauge the efficacy of the treatment."

The very word Mrs. Davies had used, and now I knew where she had heard it first. Strangely, that both reassured and dismayed me. He wasn't treating me any differently than any number of women. Therefore, the humor he'd shared with me, as though inviting me into his confidence, wasn't special at all.

Rather than think about how foolish I was, I concentrated on the sensations he produced, the warmth that built beneath the stir of his fingertips, the deep curling desperation in my womb.

The nozzle was lowered to just above my sex, and then he turned the ring at the base that released the water. The more he turned it, the narrower the stream and the harsher the pulse that beat against my love knot.

He made no sound, asked no questions, but must have read my expression, because he adjusted it back to a gentle pulse that excited but didn't make me squirm.

He rose and walked around me, eyeing me from different angles, his hand coming down to touch the pulse throbbing at the side of my throat and pull the fabric taut against my breasts. "I do have a purpose," he said. "Although your breasts seem lovely, I'm merely gauging the depth of your arousal by the reaction of your nipples."

"What does one have to do with the other?" I asked, although the question was disingenuous. I knew full well that when I played with my breasts, I felt as though a thin, internal rope tugged my sex into arousal.

"Are you really so unaware?" he said softly.

I lifted my chin. "I'm not married."

"But twenty-three and as well-formed as you are, I can't imagine you've never felt a man's embrace."

"It's awkward talking about intimate things like that just now."

"Because what I am doing is so very intimate?"

"That's precisely why it's awkward."

He shrugged. "I must gauge your breasts directly. Is that clinical enough for you? I have a device that will deliver a pleasant vibration to stimulate them."

"The clamps? They aren't painful? I know that Mrs. Smith grimaced when you applied them."

"And you stayed to watch her silently thrash upon the table. Did she appear to be in pain?"

"Of course not." Although her rapture had been a nearly painful thing to watch. I'd had to concentrate on watching the dials rather than the churning of her body.

I pulled down the neckline of the gown until the gathered edge rode beneath my breasts. The tips were engorged. When his fingers twirled on the stems, I dug my fingers into the padded squabs.

"You don't have to muzzle your cries. In fact, they'll help me determine the course of your treatment."

Freed, I moaned. The sensations he wrung from me, with the warmth pulsing between my legs, the crimping of my nipples, were already richer than anything I'd ever managed on my own.

Clamps were set, one at a time, on the tips of my breasts. Then he left me to throw up the lever. A humming vibration traveled through the wires delivering the faintest of electrical currents.

"Astounding," I gasped.

"Isn't it?" he said, his eyes lighting with enthusiasm. "I had to experiment for the longest time to find just the right amount of current."

"Who did you find to serve as your subject?" I asked, wondering who had dared to put themselves at risk. But then again, here I sat, my nipples receiving electrical charges, my sex exposed to the lash of warm streams of water. "This is all very..."

"Stimulating?"

I snorted, an unladylike action, but one that only made him grin.

"The hydropathy machine wasn't my own invention. I merely perfected the delivery system. This next device wasn't my idea either, but I have worked with metal molds to conform the seat to a woman's anatomy, improving the sensations."

The nozzle was turned off, and I missed the water, which had produced a sensual lethargy that made it impossible for me to stand against any suggestion the doctor might make. "What is the next device?"

"A vibrating saddle."

"Like a horse's saddle?"

"No, you don't ride it, it rides you."

The split in the table was raised then shortened to allow my legs to dangle from the knee. My thighs were pushed farther apart. The position alone made my breath hitch. Everything was open for him to see. And he looked. His fingers touched the delicate furls of my inner labia then probed gently inside. His thumb caressed the knot that was fully exposed now and so swollen I wondered if it were possible for it to burst like a ripe berry.

His lambent gaze rose to greet mine. "You will like this, I think."

He pulled down an oval object at the end of a flexible arm that extended from the ceiling and pushed it toward my open thighs. The head of the device was contoured to a woman's sex. A long, ruffled ridge slid between my folds, a slight protrusion anchored it at my entrance without invading so far it might steal my virtue. Straps were buckled around my upper thighs to hold it in place. When it lay against me, the metal quickly heated. The doctor threw another lever and the device shivered and shook, the hum deafening, which was a good thing because my moans came loudly, one atop the other, although the frantic thrashing of my head had to give him enough response to gauge the efficacy of this particular treatment.

My whole body shuddered. My hips danced upon the table, shoving my sex against the device, which did no good at all since the straps made it move with me. "Doctor, there's a flaw in the design," I gasped.

"Is there now, Nurse Percy?"

"I cannot...thrust against it..."

"Why don't you hold it against you?"

My gaze met his as I grasped the sides of the vibrating saddle and hugged it against my core. I ground and ground but fell back against the table breathing hard and feeling discouraged because I didn't think I had reached culmination. I wasn't cooing like a dove. I felt ready to spit and claw like a lioness.

"My dear, you are a difficult case," he murmured. "But I am determined to prove that I'm not a fraud. You have two choices. You can allow me to give you a manual pelvic massage or you can help me test my new invention." His gaze slid to the tarp.

Mine followed. "I really shouldn't let you give me a direct pelvic massage," I said, faintly. "When questioned by any suitor, I wouldn't want to lie about the fact that I found my pleasure with another man's hands." When my gaze returned, his smile stretched.

"Very admirable, nurse. The machine it is." He undid the straps at my thighs, lowered the spread platforms and helped me to my feet. The gown fell down around me, cloaking me, but I didn't care. It was only a sop to my modesty. I liked the way his glance raked my form, lingering on my breasts and the apex of my thighs.

"I couldn't help but notice when I probed you that your hymen isn't intact. It's not unusual in virgin women, but it's convenient for our purposes because you will be able to truth-fully tell your future suitor that no man's member has ever entered your body."

I quivered at the implication.

He drew the tarp from the low-lying contraption and I eyed it, not understanding its use. There was a padded bench and a wand attached to a machine that pointed toward the bench.

My expression must have given away my confusion.

"Perhaps you'll understand if I add one of these." He fished into a drawer at the foot of the bench, where inside lay an array of phallic-shaped ornaments. He selected the smallest and screwed it onto the end of the wand.

Understanding at last, my knees went weak. "Do you have a name for your device?" I rasped.

"I do. However, I'll have to find a delicate one when I add it to the menu of treatments I offer my patients."

"What do you call it now?"

"I call it a fucking machine."

The word made my nipples spike hard.

"When I start the engine, this wand will piston forward and back, mimicking the motion of a man's hips as he drives into a woman." His gaze turned from his treasure to me. "Only this machine will never erupt prematurely, depriving the woman of her culmination, and the strength of the thrusts are controlled by the woman as well, so that she can select what pleases her."

"What must I do?"

"Nothing, my dear. Bend over the bench. I will do the rest."

The look in his eyes, at once excited for his new invention and curious whether I would comply, made me nervous. I saw no straps on this device. "If I wish to move away after it begins...?"

"Look over the edge of bench."

I bent and spotted a dial marked "Speed" and another marked "Depth". I twisted both to the lowest settings but didn't touch the toggle switch to turn it on. Control truly would rest in my own hands. I cleared my throat. "Must you watch?"

"However will I determine if it requires adjustment?"

I stiffened my spine against his crestfallen expression. However attractive the man was, the position I would take before this device would rob me of my dignity. "Can't I make a record of my experiences?"

He sighed, but nodded his head. "To adjust the height of the wand, use this turnkey." He bent and whirled the wand up and down.

I frowned. "Adjusting it correctly might prove awkward and time-consuming." I knelt on the bench then rested on the padded platform. "Would you place it for me and then leave?"

"Of course, my dear." He inched up the gown over my buttocks, exposing me. "I'll just lubricate the phallus with a little ointment." Moist sounds were followed by a whirring while he rolled the wand up and down, then forward so that it touched my woman's furrow. "You've the dials turned low?"

"Yes," I said, breathless now and feeling a little intimidated. "What if something goes wrong?"

"It's experimental—in its testing phase. It is possible."

"Perhaps..." I bit my lip.

"I'll face away," he said quickly, "unless you call out to me."

"I don't think that's necessary. I'm over my bout of embarrassment."

"Wonderful! How brave you are, dear. You have only to flip the switch now."

I swallowed hard and reached for the toggle, and as soon as I did the phallus pressed slowly forward, entering me. I jerked in alarm and turned off the switch. I gave a strangled laugh. "Sorry, I knew what would happen, but the sensation..."

"You are inexperienced. Nervousness is to be expected."

I closed my eyes and backed up to the phallus again then flipped the toggle. This time, I didn't demur when it pressed inside me. It only swept forward an inch or two before retreating, but the swelling I'd experienced earlier when I was aroused returned quickly. The phallus came into me again and moisture leaked to anoint its head.

"Oh, my," I said, slumping against the bench.

The doctor knelt in front of me, his gaze locking with mine. "I think you can take so much more, Nurse Percy. Your treatment is progressing nicely."

"Indeed. Would you?" I said, waving at the dials.

He turned them, increasing the speed and depth then hurried to the rear of the platform. "I'll want you to remember everything to document your impressions."

I was glad he wasn't watching my face because I rolled my eyes. The phallus thrust fast and with remarkable precision, but I found I couldn't move, couldn't thrash like I wanted to in order to relieve my tension. "Doctor?"

"Yes, dear?"

"The machine works quite nicely, but I don't think I will culminate. Perhaps it's just me."

"There's nothing wrong with you." He hurried around the front of the machine and turned it off. "Turn and sit at the edge of the bench."

I did so, spreading my legs at his touch. Then he licked the tips of his fingers and thrust two inside me while he rubbed my love knot.

"You may move and make noises. I love the song a woman sings when she culminates."

"I'm tone deaf."

His chuckle warmed me, and I followed my impulse and tweaked my nipples through my gown. He growled, his fingers thrust deeper, and the swirling created an intense sensation that had me lifting my legs to fold them over the doctor's shoulders while I lay back on the padded bench.

My breasts and belly tightened, my channel convulsed. "Doctor!"

I culminated, my body writhing, my legs drawing the doctor closer until he braced his arms on the bench as he leaned over me. When the explosions rippling through me muted, I panted and opened my eyes to find him smiling softly down at me.

When I could find my voice, I said, "I'm sorry that I didn't have patience to prove the efficacy of your new machine."

"Not to worry, Nurse Percy," he drawled. "We will continue our experiment. I have several new ideas to test."

"May I offer a few suggestions for improvements, sir?"

His blue eyes glinted with pleasure. "My machines await your pleasure, my dear."

HER OWN DEVICES

Lisabet Sarai

A whisper of silk; a faint click of wooden heels against the paving stones: Lin Xiao Chung strode along Des Voeux Road as swiftly and silently as voluminous skirts and breath-stealing corset allowed. During the day this street would be clogged with pushcarts and carriages but now, on the cusp of midnight, Lin encountered no one. She had released the chair and bearers near Central Market in order to continue on foot. Lin was on the master's business—delicate business—and the fewer souls who knew, the better.

Mist haloed the gas flames that lit her flickering way. A sticky fog rose from the harbor, redolent of rotting fish and human waste. Lin ignored the familiar stench, turning uphill onto Chiu Lung Road. Orange lantern-light filtered from the shuttered stalls. Incense from family shrines sweetened the air. As she crossed Queens Road, a carriage clattered by. Her slender form melted into the shadows of a doorway.

Lin scanned the empty thoroughfare through her veil,

concentrating on slowing the heart that beat frantically under her snug bodice. A sliver of moon glimmered overhead. Lin murmured a quick prayer to Chang'e, asking for help in her venture. One gloved hand strayed to the blade belted under her tablier overskirt. It was always advisable to be prepared.

The moon disappeared, blotted out by a giant airship on its way to the dirigible port in Repulse Bay. The bulbous craft sailed over Victoria Peak and out of view in a matter of seconds. Lin's brows knotted into a frown. Christopher Burton's revolutionary hybrid engine had cut the England to China voyage from months to weeks—for military as well as civilian purposes. Every day now, the British tightened their hold on the Imperial throat.

Lin didn't really care about politics. Now, however, Burton had applied his engineering genius on a more intimate scale, threatening her master's fortunes. This concerned her very much indeed.

She paused before the granite façade of Burton's house, catching her breath. According to the master's spies, the butler and housekeeper should both be off duty this evening. Burton was reportedly a strange creature, unlike the other white barbarians. Despite his enormous wealth, he kept only a small staff. He preferred hiking the scrubby, solitary hills of the island to the balls and card parties frequented by the other English. It was rumored that he was fluent in the dialects of both Canton and Peking.

Lin brushed the dust off her gown and arranged her features into a mask of composure. The doorbell echoed in the bowels of the house and, after a moment, the heavy door swung open.

"Well, then! What a delicious surprise! What brings you to my threshold so late, my pretty?"

The figure in the portal was shorter than the average Englishman Lin had met, clean-shaven, with cropped silvery hair. Brilliant blue eyes burned in a tanned, mostly unlined face. A broad smile revealed unusually white, even teeth. Despite the hearty friendliness—indeed, the inappropriate informality—of Burton's greeting, Lin sensed a challenge, a wariness that fit with her knowledge of Burton's checkered history.

The owner of the house wore well-fitting wool trousers and waistcoat, his shirt open at the collar and rolled up to just below the elbow. Lin noticed a gold loop piercing one shapely ear. The rumors were true. This was no gentleman.

Lin's English was precise, with only the faintest trace of an accent. "Please accept my apologies for disturbing you at such a late hour, sir, but I wish to confer with you on a private matter. May I enter?"

"Of course. Please. Where are my manners?" He stood aside, making a gesture of welcome. "Come into my parlor. I was just reading and enjoying some sherry, which I would be delighted to share. My servants are off tonight, however. We will be completely alone. I hope that you are not overly concerned for your reputation."

Lin could not miss the mockery in his voice. Of course no respectable woman would show up on a strange man's doorstep in the middle of the night. Drawing herself to her full height, Lin gathered her skirts and hustled past him, through the shadowy hall and through a set of double doors into the warmly lit space opposite the entry.

The parlor offered a peculiar jumble of Eastern and Western elements. A daguerreotype of the English queen hung over the mantel. Stiff-looking mahogany armchairs with scrolled legs sat on an exquisite Mongolian carpet with a peach-blossom motif. A chaise upholstered with golden dragons stretched under the windows, which were draped in burgundy velvet. Matching curtains hid a portion of the opposing wall. In one corner reared a bronze horse; another sheltered a porcelain figure of Kwan Yin. The wall between them was lined with shelves, crammed with books and various exotic items: a bleached animal skull; an enameled egg; a carved and painted mask; a dagger sheathed in silver filigree; a clay tablet scored with hieroglyphs. A marble-topped table near the cold hearth was cluttered with pieces of gleaming brass—gears, springs and tiny bellows—along with a loupe and some tools. Sharing the wall with the stern portrait of Victoria Regina were several erotic Indian prints whose explicitness made even Lin blush. She suspected that the juxtaposition was deliberate.

Burton followed her into the parlor, closing the doors behind them. "Please, make yourself comfortable." He gestured toward a chair. Lin deliberately completed a circuit of the room before seating herself as indicated. She removed her bonnet and gloves, placing both on a side table that already held a miniature orrery, an alabaster bowl and an opium pipe.

"Some sherry, my dear?" Burton's eyes sparkled. Clearly he was enjoying this mystery visit.

"Do you have anything stronger?" Lin met his gaze with a boldness no lady would ever adopt.

"I've rum, gin and some exceptional scotch whiskey." Her host was already opening a cabinet next to the fireplace that held several decanters.

"Whiskey, if you please."

"Whatever madam desires," answered Burton, scarcely able to keep the glee from his voice. He had to be in his fifties, but he moved like a much younger man, lithe and sure, as he poured amber liquid into two glasses and placed one in her hand. He took a chair opposite her and sipped at his drink. Lin did the same, savoring the delicious burn as the liquor slipped down her throat.

For long moments each took the other's measure. Lin realized her objectives might be more difficult to achieve than she had expected. He was devilishly attractive. It would be hard to maintain control.

Chris Burton surveyed the luscious visitor. She was taller than most of the girls Burton employed, but had the same willowy grace. Her jet hair was gathered into a knot at her nape, fastened by a carved ivory pin that Burton's fingers itched to remove. Her fashionable silk frock spoke of wealth and taste. It hid the details of her figure but suggested pleasing curves. Her eyes were a surprising green and her nose was more prominent than most Chinese; perhaps she was of mixed blood.

She was waiting for her host to speak. Burton was willing to offer a small surrender.

"So what business is this that has brought you to my door so late, my dear?"

Her eyes hardened to points of jade. "My name is Lin. Lin Xiao Chung. My master is the illustrious Fang Wu."

Burton knew the name—a rich merchant with pretensions to nobility, who also happened to operate the most exclusive brothels on the island. The most exclusive, that is, until Burton had arrived.

"Master Wu's reputation precedes him although I do not have the honor of his acquaintance." Though they were conversing in English, Burton fell automatically into the polite formulas of Chinese discourse. "I cannot imagine how a humble foreigner such as I could assist him."

The girl blinked twice before answering. "Let us speak frankly, Mr. Burton. Since you arrived in Hong Kong, Fang Wu's business has suffered greatly. Many of his regular customers, both foreign and native, have deserted his houses for your establishment."

"My establishment?" Burton pretended innocence, just for the fun of it.

"Your brothel, sir." Lin flushed. Burton smiled in encouragement. "The House of the White Tiger. People whisper about the marvelous sex machines you offer, cunning devices contrived for pleasure or punishment. Your engines supposedly make previously existing sexual mechanisms look primitive and crude."

"Well, that is the nature of commerce, is it not, Miss Lin? Competition is fundamental and superior technology will usually triumph."

"My master will not be satisfied with this answer. He would like to purchase your technology. Name your price."

Burton laughed. "I have no need of money. Surely Master Wu must know this."

"Why, then, do you persist in depriving him of his rightful income?"

"His rightful income? Well, I don't know about that. You Chinese know better than anyone that business is war. He has to earn his money, just as I do. As for me, I'll be honest—I opened the White Tiger for my own entertainment. And of course as a way to annoy the merchants and dowagers of polite Hong Kong society." Not to mention arrogant Han bandits like Wu, the entrepreneur added mentally.

Lin sat silent, twisting her hands in her lap. Burton wondered what Wu would do to her, if she failed in her mission. "Show me," she said, finally. "Show me your machines."

"Would you like a demonstration? That can be arranged."

"Not—not now," she answered coolly. Her poise was remarkable. "I merely want to be able to explain to my master why your house is so popular. Surely you must have models on the premises."

"I can do better than exhibit models, my dear. I can show you the devices in action."

Burton rose and drew open the curtains that draped the south wall. Lin's gasp was more than sufficient reward for revealing a few secrets.

"What—how?" The comely visitor stepped closer to the wall, staring at the round panels of glass embedded in the surface, rather like the portholes on a steamship. Each port displayed some lascivious scene.

In one window, a cloud of feathers pulsed around several naked forms writhing on a divan. With each thrust, the downy plumes caressed and tickled the bare skin of the two—or was it three?—participants. The feathers seemed alive, their motions triggered by cunning sensors in the divan itself.

Another port displayed a lean mandarin, wearing only the hat that signified his office. A nude woman knelt at his feet. Each time she bent her head to swallow the man's erection, a machine behind him lashed him with leather thongs, raining fierce blows down on his shoulders and back. His mouth twisted in a grimace that could have signified pain or pleasure.

"She controls the beating by squeezing her thighs together," Burton murmured in Lin's ear. "Pneumatics. Works nicely during copulation as well." The girl's breath came faster. Clearly Burton's creations had an arousing effect even at a distance.

In a window in the center rank, a delicate Chinese woman was bound naked on a wrought iron frame. Beside her, a corpulent, bewhiskered Englishman ran his hands over a keyboard. As he played, phallus-shaped rods plunged into or emerged from the prisoner's mouth, quim and bum, apparently in time to some unheard music. Pincers on jointed arms plucked at the girl's nipples and little animated needles pricked the swell of her breasts.

"There's a plug up the major's arse, too," Burton commented. "And a sleeve on his cock. He's always fancied himself a musician...."

"How is this possible?" Lin tore her gaze away from the silent tableaux of lust to confront their creator. "The House of the White Tiger is two miles from here."

Burton shrugged. "Lenses. Mirrors. Conduits lined with glass." Her musky scent wafted up from under her skirts and petticoats. She must be extremely aroused. "I've installed some ports in the house itself, of course. As you might expect, many of my clients enjoy watching the games being played in other chambers."

Lin's eyes blazed with green fire. "This is outrageous! Obscene!"

"I take that as a compliment, Miss Lin." Burton grinned. What a savory morsel she was!

"I must have these things. My master must have them." Her earnestness only made her more desirable. "If money does not sway you, then I offer you my person. You are known to be a lustful man, highly susceptible to the charms of female flesh. You may perpetrate any sort of carnal act that pleases you upon my body. I will not resist."

Burton circled her waist and pulled her tight. Her heart beat like a trapped bird under the ruffled silk of her bodice. "Ah, but will you enjoy it, Miss Lin? And do you think that a single coupling would be adequate recompense for sharing the fruits of my engineering labors?"

Lin would not meet his eyes. "I am the slave of Master Wu," she murmured, so soft that Burton could scarcely hear. "In return for the keys to your devices, my master will gift me to you. Permanently."

Burton brought their lips together for a moment. Her breath

smelled of ginger. "I don't need a slave, Lin. All I need is a willing partner." Her breasts were soft pillows swelling above the rigid constraints of her stays. Her stiff, fat nipples could be detected even through the layers of her chemise, bodice and tunic vest.

"I want you, Lin. Do you want me?" Chris Burton already knew the answer, but wanted to hear it from her own lips.

"Yes," she sighed, leaning against the engineer's chest as though weak with desire. "I do."

Burton snatched the ivory ornament from her chignon. A flood of midnight hair cascaded down her back.

Lin's corset gripped her torso like an iron cage. She could scarcely breathe. Burton undressed her with unexpected skill, seeming to understand all the intricacies of female couture. With deftness and patience he undid the hooks, buttons and laces that held her elaborate costume together. He did not pause to caress her, but each time his fingers brushed her bare skin, she trembled. There was no need for her to feign excitement as was often the case when she serviced Master Wu or his guests. In a delicious swoon, she submitted to Burton's ministrations.

She remembered the hidden knife at the very last minute, snatching the tablier from his hands just as he untied it. She set the garment on the table flanking the chaise. Burton raised an eyebrow but said nothing, continuing to remove her vest, bodice, skirt and petticoat.

He turned her around like a doll and buried his face in her hair, breathing her scent while kneading her buttocks through her cambric knickers. Without thinking she arched back, rubbing her bum against his groin. The hardness she detected there set off a flood in her quim. He slid one hand around her waist and down her belly to cup her mound. She moaned, spreading her thighs, inviting him within. Burton chuckled and strummed his fingers against the damp fabric, making her jerk in his grasp.

"I observe that you are quite ready for my attentions," he said. "But let's get rid of this bloody corset first." Sweeping her hair over her shoulder, he addressed himself to the laces criss-crossing her back, loosening them until there was sufficient give to release the front hooks on the garment. Air rushed into Lin's lungs. She stumbled against him, momentarily dizzy.

Burton caught her and lowered her to the chaise. Then he removed her pantaloons, leaving her naked but for her chemise and silk stockings.

The lust Lin saw in his eyes reminded her of who she was and why she was there. She reclined against the golden cushions, her hair fanning out behind her. She knew that she was irresistible. Bringing her heels up onto the couch, she opened her thighs to expose her moist pink cleft. The humid scent of her sex filled the parlor. "Take me, sir," she entreated, her voice husky. "I'm yours."

She expected Burton to tear open his trousers and plunge his manhood into her tempting wetness. Instead, he knelt between her splayed legs. His warm breath danced over her sensitive tissues. Her nipples tightened into aching knots. Fresh liquid trickled into the creases of her bent legs.

For ages he did nothing but blow gently into her quim. She squirmed, tilting her pelvis toward his face, striving vainly for contact. Arousal and frustration wiped everything else from her mind. "Please..." she begged, all pride forgotten.

Burton used his tongue to answer, sweeping long strokes from the back of her quim to the front, flicking briefly over the nub hidden at the apex each time he arrived there. Each touch stoked the embers of her pleasure. Each flick made delight flare. She writhed under his mouth, wanting more, and he was merciful. He buried his face in her slick folds, using lips, tongue and teeth to drive her into a frenzy. First he'd suck on her whorled flesh, then he'd poke his tongue deep into her hollows, waking an irresistible desire for penetration; then he'd stab at her swollen pearl, worrying it back and forth until she moaned uncontrollably.

Lin never reached climax with her customers, but she felt a crisis gathering now, bearing down upon her like a runaway steam engine. The heat and the pressure climbed to unbearable levels. Burton focused on her clit now, sucking and nibbling, while one hand frigged her quim and the other toyed with her bum-hole. She fought against her body, unwilling to lose control, but the master engineer between her thighs manipulated her like some clockwork automaton. He knew which levers to throw, which buttons to push. When he nipped at her pearl and pushed two fingers into her bum, she flew off into climax, wheeling helplessly through sparkling inner space.

The next thing Lin knew, Burton was on the chaise, looming over her limp body. A cock of very respectable size protruded from his unbuttoned trousers, with a moist pink bulb that made her mouth water. He rubbed the tip over the still-twitching flesh of her quim. Lin smiled and spread her thighs wide, inviting him inside.

The warm, smooth rod of flesh felt wonderful sliding into her climax-sensitized depths. He moved gracefully between her legs, stroking in and out with a firm, steady rhythm completely unlike the rough prodding most men employed. She clutched at him with well-trained muscles and felt his flesh ripple in response, swelling to fill her more completely. Hands on her knees, he urged her thighs farther apart so that he could penetrate more deeply.

Ah, this was delicious! A new climax stirred in her belly, coiling tighter with each of his strokes. Burton was watching her, reading her reactions with those bright blue eyes. She cupped her breasts and tugged on the nipples, knowing this would excite him, finding that it excited her as well. He moved faster, plunging into her with greater force, just as she craved. Her climax bubbled up, nearing the surface. He slammed into her again and again. Each stroke carried her a breath closer to orgasm.

His eyes were closed now. His fingernails dug into her flesh but the slight pain only took her higher. He bit down on his lip as his hips jerked, driving his cock into her flesh. He was striving, reaching for release the same way she was.

All at once he gave a funny, high-pitched yell and ground his pelvis against hers. Wet heat billowed inside her as he filled her with his spunk. The sensation pushed her over the edge and then she was coming too, spasming around his hardness, colors flashing behind her eyes.

Lin recovered before Burton. She found him slumped against the wall, eyes shut and mouth open. His cock protruded from his trousers, slick with cunt-juice and come, but still as hard as ever—or perhaps hard again. The sight rekindled her uncharacteristic lust. She clambered over to his prone form and bent to kiss his lovely rampant organ.

The taste was—strange. She recognized the flavor of her own secretions, but there was none of the chalky bitterness of a man's seed. And the skin—it was as soft as it looked but far more elastic than it should have been. It was almost rubbery. Nevertheless, the organ twitched and swelled in response to her attentions.

Lin slipped a stealthy hand into Burton's trousers, exploring his odd genitals. She traced the smooth length of the shaft down toward the man's belly, expecting wiry hair and the twin sacs of his balls.

Instead she encountered canvas straps, soft down and the unmistakable slickness of a woman's pussy.

A fingertip brushing her clit roused Chris Burton from her post-coital lethargy. She moaned in delight before bolting upright. "What in bloody hell do you think you're doing?" Her strong fingers clamped down on Lin's wrist and dragged the invading hand out of her trousers.

Lin's jade eyes were wide with shock. She didn't even attempt to free herself. "You're—you're a woman!"

"So?" A ghost of Burton's trademark grin illuminated her face. "I still made you come, did I not? Twice, if I am not mistaken."

"But your cock—it felt so real. It reacted to my motions just like a man's. I felt it swelling. I felt it pumping."

"Just clever clockwork, my dear." Burton pushed her trousers down to her ankles to display a bewildering array of tubes and wires connected to the still-engorged phallus. "A tiny steam engine fed by my body heat. Electrostatic sensors. Pneumatic systems for fluid delivery and hydraulics for motion."

"You are a genius," said Lin, admiration evident in her voice.

"You're right. I am." Burton pulled off the rest of her clothing and stood naked before the still-astounded Chinese woman. Chris Burton was sturdily built, with muscular thighs, small breasts sporting nipples the size of pennies and ample hips that had been hidden by her male garb. A pale scar crossed her chest from left shoulder to her sternum, souvenir of one of her more dangerous voyages. Another marred her belly. Her pubic hair was as silver as the pelt on her head. She shrugged and smiled wryly. "But what good does it do me when I can't be myself?"

"What do you mean?"

"I've been masquerading as male most of my life. My parents succumbed to typhoid in Rajastan when I was twelve. I knew that I'd have to become a boy to survive and to do all the things I wanted to do. I have had forty years of adventures: expeditions, inventions, seductions. Lately, though, wearing the mask has become a bit tiresome."

"And has no one ever discovered the truth before?" Burton could see the wheels turning in Lin's brain. She grabbed the Chinese girl's arm and twisted it to the back, pulling the scantily clad body tight against her own.

"No one who lived." With her other hand, Burton reached for Lin's overskirt. She fished out the knife and traced the tip along Lin's cheek. "I can't trust anyone to keep my secret. So there have been a few who have carried it to the grave."

"You can trust me." Chris Burton heard the pleading in Lin's voice. The girl reached back with her free hand, trying to stroke Burton's breast.

"Oh, really? Then why were you carrying a hidden blade?" Burton whirled the younger woman around, catching both wrists in one powerful hand while holding the knife to Lin's throat with the other.

Lin looked remarkably composed despite her danger. Her brow was unlined and her eyes were tranquil, verdant pools. "The knife was purely to protect myself, I swear. I walked here, by myself. I might have encountered some villain who wanted my purse or my honor."

"Your honor!" Burton chuckled grimly. "The honor of a whore?"

Lin did not flinch. "Furthermore, I might have needed a weapon to use against you. After all, a woman alone with a strange man..."

"Did you not come here intending to seduce me?"

"That was just one option... Please, let me go. I won't tell anyone."

"Hmph!" Burton gave a skeptical grunt, but she released Lin nevertheless. The oriental beauty sank down onto the chaise. "What about your precious Master Wu?"

"I hate him." Lin's voice was full of venom. "Until I met you, though, I had no other option but to obey him."

"And now? What do you propose? How will you satisfy him that you have fulfilled his commission?"

"He really did offer me to you as your slave."

"He must be quite desperate to get hold of my inventions." Chris Burton lowered herself to the carpet, where she crossed her legs Indian style.

"Oh, he is. He's obsessed with you. The 'devil engineer' he calls you."

Burton grinned. "I like that. It fits."

"I don't think he realizes what a true genius you are. I certainly did not. I would wager that you come up with new ideas for carnal machines all the time."

"Oh, I do. If you only knew...."

"So give him your current inventions. Last year's models, if you will. Then set your mind to devising the next generation of erotic technology." Lin's delicate fingers hovered like humming-birds above Burton's bare skin. "I can help you."

Burton grabbed the fluttering hand and kissed Lin's palm. "Oh? How will you help?"

Lin slipped off the chaise into Burton's lap. "You can test them all on me." She pursed her lips around one of Burton's nipples. The older woman squirmed. "And Chris—may I call you that?"

"Christine," Burton replied. The long-unused name was strange on her tongue.

"You can be yourself with me, Christine. You don't have to pretend. You can take off your trousers and vest and be a woman again." Lin's nimble fingers slithered into Christine's quim. "We could even travel together—a wealthy widow and her young secretary."

Christine flipped Lin onto her back and straddled her, rubbing the artificial phallus back and forth in the girl's slick crease. "Or we could travel as men. That would give us a lot more freedom. I could build you a clockwork cock of your own and teach you to use it. I could use my cock to take you like the boy you were pretending to be. Would you like that?" Lin's eyes grew wide when the infernal device impaled her. She nodded, gasping, as Christine began to stroke.

"Yes, Lin—I think we're on the brink of a brave new world."

LAIR OF THE
RED COUNTESS

Kathleen Bradean

An inch of ash flaked off Archibald Fraser's cigar and dropped onto the back of the snarling tiger splayed at his feet. He glanced around the oak-paneled public room of the Adventurer's Club and settled back into his chair as he stifled a sigh. When he'd been home, an urgent need to get out had driven him to the club, but once there, he found himself in a similar state.

The moment Archie had entered the club, the squire had attached himself with the tenacity of a leech. It was widely acknowledged, though never mentioned in the squire's hearing, that he hadn't set foot outside London in a decade. While the squire admired adventurers tremendously and relished dressing like one, he was deeply suspicious of clean air and plants that hadn't been sculpted into topiary. The little Egyptian adventure he was so fond of retelling had either taken place twenty years ago, or, more likely, was cobbled together from the exploits of members of the club who had actually been there.

Toffy (Edmund "Toffy" Toffington, Third Earl of Stoke-On-Trent) bounded into the room and took the chair beside Archie. When he saw the squire, he began to rise, but then plopped back into place, resigned to his fate.

As the squire droned on, Archie sipped his whiskey and stared at the fire. He had no obligations in town. Perhaps he should simply board a train and head off somewhere. Just where, he had no idea. He smoothed his magnificent ginger moustache as he tried to decide. Scotland? No. France? No.

"Archie, I say, what do you think of that?" Toffy asked.

Archie hated to admit that he hadn't been listening attentively. "Frightful," he said.

"It is! If I wanted to see my wife, I'd go home."

Archie realized Toffy had been talking about something other than the squire's alleged Egyptian adventure. "Sorry. My mind was elsewhere. What's this about Lady Toffington?"

"She's joined that new Spiritualist's Society. Bunch of damned women talking to spirits. Bad enough that she's holding séances in our home, but now she's visiting their club all the time, and it's right across the street!"

"You don't say." Archie wasn't married, so he wasn't aware of how inconvenient it could be to run into one's wife in public.

"You're awfully quiet this evening, Archie. Touch of Amazon fever?"

The truth was that Archie was bored. He'd been bored before he set out to South America, was fitful while he was there and had suffered a bit of melancholia upon returning to London. The problem, he decided, was that no matter where he went, he remained the same.

"Are you dining here at the club tonight?" the squire asked.

"Er..." Toffy glanced at Archie.

Archie set his cigar on the elephant foot table beside his

chair. "Maybe you're right about Amazon fever. Can't seem to hold still." Even as he said it, he felt how true it was. He couldn't stay where he was for another moment. "Maybe I'll go check out that Spiritualist's Club."

The squire gasped. "But all those women."

"A bit of adventure." Archie winked at Toffy.

Toffy grabbed a newspaper and held it before his face. "If you see my wife, don't tell her where I am."

Alerted by the slam of the Adventurer's Club's door, a crossing sweeper ran ahead of Archie to clear a path through the horse dung and street filth. When they reached the establishment across the street without a befouling incident, the urchin raised his hand for his penny. Archie tossed it to him and mounted the stone stairs.

Feeling that he was being watched, Archie looked over his shoulder at the Adventurer's Club. The curtains in the front window jerked closed. He harrumphed and turned back to the red door before him.

A stout hall porter answered the bell. "May I help you, sir?"

Archie shouldered past the man. "I wish to speak to the person in charge of this establishment."

"I'm afraid that most of the members are attending a séance in Kensington." The hall porter closed the door and followed Archie into the foyer. He extended his hand for Archie's hat, but was rebuffed.

"Nonsense. Someone must be here." Archie figured that the worst that could happen was that he'd be thrown out of the place. He almost welcomed such a scene. It would be something different, after all.

A staircase immediately ahead of Archie lead to the upper stories of the narrow townhouse. Oriental rugs covered the black-and-white marble floor of the foyer. Double doors immediately to his right were closed.

Archie pulled open the doors and stepped into a room he imagined was a parlor. The gas lamps were turned so low that it was hard to see. A round table covered by a fringed cloth sat before the fireplace. As his eyes grew accustomed to the twilight, he saw chairs and settees whose deep cushions were upholstered in jewel-tone velvets. Every small table in the room was crowded with pictures and knickknacks. It was a distinctly feminine room, but then, the spiritualist movement was largely composed of, and led by, women. He snorted. Every occultist he'd met on his adventures understood the importance of atmosphere. What the frilly room needed, he thought, was a mummified monkey's paw and a few skulls.

The whisper of silk skirts close by caught Archie's attention. He turned, and immediately his eyes were drawn to the luminescent orbs of a magnificent bosom, which, like twin moons, crested at a thin horizon of black lace. The woman those orbs were attached to sat in a leather wingback chair. She wore a dress of such deep garnet silk that she was almost swallowed whole by the shadows except for the ethereal luminescence of her décolletage.

Archie's ruminations on the efficacy of sliding his suddenly turgid cock between those orbs were interrupted by a heavily accented woman's voice that rang through the room like a whip crack.

"Even if we had been properly introduced, I would find your behavior wholly unacceptable."

Archie flinched even as his cock sprang to full attention. It was as if he'd been transported back to his first year at university, when an upstairs maid in his dean's service had taken much the same offense to his attentions. The maid spent the better part of the school year educating him in the proper expression of his base desires. Alas, during one of her afternoon tutoring sessions, his yelps had been heard, and the maid was summarily dismissed. His dean had made it quite clear that sort of thing simply wasn't done, unless, of course, it was the pert bottom of the young lady on the receiving end of the blows. With his academic career off to a tenuous start, Archie avoided further dealings with the fairer sex. Scandal was to be avoided at any cost.

"Who are you?" the woman asked. That time, her low voice caressed the nape of Archie's neck like incense smoke wreathing a sinner's prayer.

Archie drew himself up. "I'm seeking the person in charge." He squinted. She sat only two feet away from him, but the features of her face were difficult to discern.

The hall porter, who had followed Archie into the parlor, bowed to the shadowy figure. "Forgive me, Countess. He shoved his way in here. I will call the footmen."

Her gloved hand lifted. At the flick of her wrist, the hall porter backed out of the room.

A tapestry footstool slammed against Archie's ankles.

"Sit."

He was at least a foot taller than she, and his travels into rugged territory kept him in peak physical shape. He'd climbed mountains, paddled through dangerous waters, dined with indigenous chieftains and slept in Bedouin tents, and yet, one word from her, and he sank onto the footstool as if a hidden force compelled him.

His knees spread in an unseemly manner. He held his hat before his groin.

She lifted her garnet skirts just enough to flash a shapely, pale ankle. Her foot rose and with a kick sent his hat rolling across the floor.

"Leave it."

Archie withdrew his hand. As his cock sent most urgent messages to his brain, he clasped his hands at his lap and tried to press his knees together.

The countess leaned forward. The sweetly resinous scent of amber and myrrh filled his nose. Her magnificent bosom was inches from his face. It strained against the tight confines of her dress and threatened to spill over the top. With great difficulty, he tore his gaze from the alluring sight, to her eyes.

Her lips curved, as if she found him amusing. Perhaps she did. His ungainly posture made it impossible to adequately hide his erection. Another emotion glinted in her dark eyes. Her foot pressed against his most delicate gentlemen's parts.

"Madam!" As he flailed about in an attempt to back away, the pressure increased.

"I did not give you permission to rise. Be still."

Archie stared at the slippered foot wedged between his thighs as if he were a bird caught in the hypnotic gaze of a snake. He huffed as any gentleman in that situation ought to, but then realized he wasn't truly outraged. He could have escaped, of course, but for the first time in months, his ennui had dissipated. If nothing else, he was going to find out what this woman was up to.

"You try my patience. State your business."

"I am Archibald Fraser."

Her chuckle gave him an uneasy feeling. "Ah, so you are Mr. Fraser. I've been expecting you."

"You have?"

The countess grasped a bell from the cluttered table beside her chair. The parlor doors banged open. Two footmen, better suited to bear baiting or dock work than their fine livery, entered the room. Archie craned his neck to look up at the mountains of muscle headed toward him.

The countess rose from her chair. "Bring the gentleman to my laboratory."

She left the room in a swish of crinoline underskirts. The scent of amber and myrrh trailed in her wake.

Archie struggled to rise from his undignified position, but the footmen clasped their meaty hands around his arms and dragged him across the plush Oriental carpet before he could. While he was fit, he was no match for the two of them. As they yanked him down the dark hallway leading to a flight of stairs, he wondered what horrors awaited him.

The countess's laboratory was below stairs. The walls were solid stone. In contrast to the murky parlor, gaslights glowed brightly at even intervals along the wall. He'd expected the bitter scent of chemicals and questionable concoctions bubbling away in glass beakers, but the far half of the room reminded him of the library in the Adventurer's Club. It was the nearer part of the room that concerned him most, though.

Before him was a large contraption of copper and wrought iron. If he had stood on his tiptoes, Archie couldn't have reached the top bar. Hinged arms swung out to both sides of the device, giving it the look of an upside-down spider. At waist level on the device, there was a padded bar before a platform. Two glass orbs sat on either side of the platform.

Beside the curious machine was a small wrought iron engine that looked a bit like a Franklin stove that had fallen over.

"Place him in the soul machine."

The footmen forced Archie across the room to the device. He dug in his heels, to no avail.

"Help!"

The Countess laughed. "The room is quite soundproof, Mr. Fraser. With the door closed, no one will hear you."

He struggled, but there was no escaping the grips on his arms. Within moments, his stomach was pressed tight to the padded bar. The footmen attached shackles to his wrists. One turned a crank on the side of the contraption. Slowly, his arms were pulled forward until he was bent at the waist, stretched out, chest down on the platform behind the padded bar. A belt went around the small of his back, forcing his midsection against the padding. He felt tugging on his legs. Before he could think of kicking, his legs were spread much as his arms were.

"You can't do this to me! I'm an Englishman."

The footmen withdrew from the room. The heavy door shut with a dishearteningly solid thud.

The Countess ran her hands over the glass orbs that sat just beyond the reach of Archie's fingertips. "Do you like my soul machine? It's been my life's work to improve it."

Despite his situation, Archie laughed. "You fancy yourself a scientist? A woman?"

"Do I seem the fanciful sort, Mr. Fraser?"

Her tone chilled his heart. She was obviously a dangerous type; intriguing, beautiful and absolutely frightening. She struck him as a formidable foe, a nemesis to be conquered, and yet, he found being at her mercy quite alluring. Despite being manhandled by her burly footmen, his erection had not wavered one bit. If anything, it was most insistent that he release it from his trousers.

Archie gathered his dignity. "Spiritualists are nothing more than frauds who bilk the credulous with their parlor tricks. Table rapping and other such amusements do not pass the test of scientific scrutiny."

"I agree."

That wasn't what he expected her to say.

"That opinion can't make you very popular around here. If

you feel that way, why do you associate with these people?" he asked.

"Very good, Mr. Fraser. Why indeed?"

Archie rather liked that little taste of praise. He had a feeling that such approval was rare.

The countess stepped back. "As you may have guessed, I am Russian. Before I left my home, I was frequently at Peterhof. There, I witnessed Rasputin's ability, with only murmured words, to stop the Tsarevitch's bleeding. He was an awful man, Rasputin. I wanted to believe the worst, that he was a charlatan, and yet, I could not deny what he was able to do. From that moment on, I devoted myself to the study of those things that can be observed but not measured. These spiritualists are the only people I've met here who are open to such research. When you're a stranger in a strange land, you take refuge where it's offered."

Archie was tempted to make a quip about strange bedfellows, but decided against it. "But no real scientist would dabble in the occult."

"You obviously don't count many scientists among your acquaintances. But I have much more in common with…" Her nearly flawless grasp of English seemed to elude her for a moment. "We are both adventurers, Mr. Fraser. You explore rivers and jungles; I, the human soul. This device allows me to observe a man's deepest hopes and desires."

He'd heard things about the Russians and their capacity for cruelty. After all, they weren't truly European and not quite civilized. Their proximity to the Oriental mind had twisted them in ways he couldn't comprehend.

"Then it's torture, is it?"

The scent of her filled his nose like opium fumes when she moved one of the device's many spider arms under the platform. He'd glimpsed a brass ring at the end of the pole before it disappeared from sight. Something pressed against Archie's groin, but it was under the platform where he couldn't see it. He felt his cock being maneuvered inside his trousers so that the ring encased it.

"I say!"

The fit was quite snug. He wished she'd removed his erection from his trousers before she'd stuffed it into the ring.

As the countess cranked a large wheel on the side of the device, Archie's hands were pulled to the glass orbs. They were cool against his heated palms.

"Are you familiar with the scientific discoveries of Mr. Tesla? A most interesting man. I hope to meet him one day. These plasma orbs are his design, although I have improved them and modified them for my own ends."

"What nefarious plan do you have in mind?"

She smiled at him a bit sadly. "You will feel tingling in your fingertips. Don't be alarmed. It's only a mild electrical current running through your shackles. It will pass through your hands to the plasma orbs. Now, this part is very important, Mr. Fraser, so I ask that you be attentive. If you raise your hands from the orbs at any time, the current will be broken, and all sensation will stop. If you place your hands back on the orbs, it will begin again. If at any time you feel you can't go on, you will admit it to me, and I will stop the device."

"So it is torture!"

"Something far worse. Something almost unbearable." She bent close to his ear and spoke as if relishing the word rolling over her tongue. "Pleasure."

The countess flipped a switch on the weird Franklin stove on the floor. It hummed.

Archie's hands tingled. They almost tickled. His gaze was drawn from the countess to the plasma orbs. Inside them, colored lightning arced from the places where his fingertips touched the glass to a center rod. It was strangely beautiful. He'd never seen anything like it. As the lightning grew in intensity, he felt vibrations over his cock.

"Oh!" He wriggled, but he was too hard to squirm out of the ring that surrounded his cock. The belt that held him to the platform allowed him to back away a few inches, but that wasn't enough. He pushed forward again. The vibrating ring seemed to grip him even tighter.

Immediately, he understood her cunning plan. It was common knowledge that women sought to drain a man's vitality through sexual congress. He had to resist her evil machinations.

"I know what you're about, and I won't let it happen," Archie told her.

She didn't speak. Her dark eyes glinted and Archie wouldn't have been surprised to see a canary feather resting on slightly parted lips.

The vibrations increased. He pulled back before thrusting through the brass ring again. Dire things were happening inside his trousers. The sensitive head of his cock rubbed against his undergarments.

He had to take his mind off the sensations.

"How did you know who I am?"

Her eyebrows arched. "I would tell you, but I feel that you are a man greatly in need of some mystery, so I will leave the explanation to your imagination."

"Why were you expecting me?"

"Because eventually, you were bound to seek me, or someone much like me. If you believe in fate, you can ascribe our meeting to it. I prefer the more logical explanation, that as my club is across the way from yours, eventually, our paths were likely to cross."

Archie pushed deep into the ring. When he felt himself reaching a dangerous condition, he pulled as far out of it as he could. He gulped in air as he fought for control.

"You monster!"

"It wasn't as if I entrapped you, Mr. Fraser. You barged into my parlor."

"Not that!" Archie tried to twist his hips, to no avail. "I mean this infernal machine of yours."

She chuckled in that low, warm voice of hers that crept down Archie's groin and seemed to caress his balls.

"But, Mr. Fraser, it's you, not I, who chose to continue the process. I told you that you might raise your hands from the orbs at any time to stop the sensation, although in your current state, I can understand why logical thought might be difficult."

A bit ashamed that he had forgotten, Archie lifted his hands half an inch from the orbs. The lightning disappeared and the vibration stopped. The tingling in his fingers remained though. He touched the orbs. The sensations started again.

"I also told you that should matters become unbearable, all you had to do was admit it to me, and I would make it stop."

Archie barely heard a word she said as he experimented with the orbs. When only his fingertips touched the glass, the vibrations were so light he barely felt them through the thick material of his trousers. Both palms wrapped around the orbs sent his hips frantically jerking as he eagerly sought the pleasure afforded by the brass ring. The combination of one palm and just the fingertips of his other hand was just about right. It felt good, but not so intense that he had to withdraw. At that pace, he thought he might be able to continue to hump the ring for another twenty minutes.

He was relishing the beginning of a long, slow stroke into the vibrating grip of the ring when suddenly everything stopped.

"No!"

He rubbed the orbs, but the lightning was gone. He thrust into the ring, but its confines were a poor substitute for the thrilling sensations it afforded only moments before.

Panting and frantic, Archie jerked back his head to glare at the countess. "What have you done?"

"You've had quite enough."

"But—"

The countess tsk-tsked like a disapproving governess. "I'm sorry, Mr. Fraser, but I must be firm about this. There is only so much current the human body can withstand per session. You've almost reached your limit."

"Just a little longer!"

She smiled sadly. "You boys always want more than is good for you. "

"Please! I was so close." Only the stiffest of upper lips could keep his moustache from quaking.

"Close to what, Mr. Fraser?"

Blushing to a deep hue, he lowered his gaze from hers. There were some things a gentleman never discussed with a lady, even if she had rubbed his crotch with her foot and placed his cock into a ring. Despite those events, he was quite sure she was a lady. Besides, weren't all of the nobility a bit mad?

His hands suddenly tingled much more forcefully than before. Purple and pinks streaks of light branched from the surface of the orbs to the center rods. The ring around his cock hummed audibly. Archie tried to touch the orbs with just his fingertips, then only one finger per hand, but the intensity of the vibration did not diminish. Just as he was ready to beg for mercy, the current switched off. He rested his chest on the platform before him and gasped.

The countess walked behind Archie. She released the belt

that held him securely to the padding. As she walked around the device to face him, her fingers trailed up his spine.

"Perhaps this will compel you to answer." She flipped the switch on the machine's engine.

Freed from the belt, Archie found he could rut with abandon when the vibrations began again. He knew he should let go of the orbs, but as each delicious second passed, he willed himself to withstand it for just another moment. It felt so good.

The countess shut off the engine.

Archie howled.

"Close to what, Mr. Fraser?"

"Please. Just a bit more. I'm so close. It's been so long."

Surprisingly, the countess seemed filled with womanly concern for him. "How long has it been, Mr. Fraser?"

"Ages." He bowed his head. "Simply ages."

She stroked his hair and murmured soothing noises. "Tell me."

Archie wanted to resist her, but when he met her gaze, she seemed so filled with understanding that he was struck with something very close to love. She had complete control over him. He was her helpless prisoner. When faced with such a situation, what could he do but pour out his heart to her?

"For years now, I haven't been able to obtain a, uh, er, gentleman's satisfaction without being thoroughly spanked. This is the first time I've come close."

She continued stroking his hair. "This is a problem for you."

"There would be a huge scandal if anyone found out."

"I can imagine."

"May I please have a few more moments with the device? Please?"

Such a gentle smile; it was a shame it meant that her answer was no. "I never lie, Mr. Fraser. When I say you've had almost as much electricity as you can take this session, I mean it. I have no desire to harm you, after all." Her gloved hand pushed away the tear that trickled down his cheek. "However, never let it be said that I lack compassion."

Archie pressed his lips to her hand. The calfskin opera glove was warm and soft under his tentative lips. He had only a moment to wonder why a lady would chose to wear gloves of such an odd material during the evening before a sudden slap stung his cheek.

"There is a small matter we must settle before you leave, Mr. Fraser. You have needlessly wasted my time. I demand..." Her hand made a gesture as if she expected it to snatch the word she sought from the cloying air of the room. "Satisfaction."

Perhaps she had a Byzantine sense of humor, but from the mischievous turn of her lips, Archie felt as if she were offering him a grand game. Damned if he didn't admire this woman. And if it meant he might relieve the urgency in his trousers, he was willing to play along.

"What fiendish torture do you have in mind, countess?"

Her eyes sparkled approval. "Something horrible." She ran her pink tongue over her obscenely plump lips as if she relished the thought of it. "Something thoroughly English."

Archie waited for her to explain. He suspected she took great delight in making him wait for the final resolution of his discomfort.

"I believe you attended public school, Mr. Fraser?"

The countess opened a cabinet beside her laboratory table. There were many intriguing devices inside, but she quickly picked one and closed the door, denying him the chance to make sense of what he saw.

The countess held a sleek cane in her gloved hands. The way she ran it over her palm was exceedingly lewd. If she didn't stop, he was going to fill his undergarments with a hefty dollop of his gentlemen's vitality.

If they were playacting, it was obviously up to him to continue the game. "I'll report you to the authorities!"

"You would be ridiculed. Isn't scandal what your fear most?" She leaned close to his ear. "After what happened at university, do you really want people to know that you were found with your bottom soundly thrashed and your penis engorged?"

"How did you—?"

She stood. As she paced, she smacked the cane against her palm. Each delicious sharp report sent shudders of anticipation through Archie's body.

Archie closed his eyes as he felt tugging on his trousers. Quickly, expertly, the countess bared his bottom. With her silk skirts pressed to his skin, she reached under the platform to move a different arm of the device under it. His bared cock was soon held in a snug tube.

She stepped back. Her warm, leather-clad hand slid over his buttocks. If only it were her ungloved hand instead. He lifted on his toes and arched his back to follow her touch.

She walked beyond Archie's field of vision.

A whoosh of air was the only warning Archie received before the cane landed on his buttocks. He screamed more from surprise than from pain. He knew that the initial sting was nothing compared to what would come. Rather than fading, the pain increased to a deep throb.

Another blow landed parallel to the first. As the pain reached a crescendo, her warm hand caressed his buttock. He wished she would keep doing that. It was comforting. The dean's maid hadn't been that solicitous of him during their sessions. While the pain and humiliation were what he craved, the affection sank into his parched soul and sated a thirst he'd never realized he had.

"This is what I enjoy about the English. You're so fair, but your bottoms turn such a lovely dark shade of pink. Have you had time to catch your breath, Mr. Fraser? Nod if the answer is yes. You only have to endure several more, this time. Further misdeeds will result in more blows. Ah, a nod. Very good."

The third blow was like a whiff of smelling salts. He rocked into the tube that encased his cock. When the forth blow came, he rutted forcefully. His balls tightened.

"That's the stuff," he muttered. "More. Please, Ma'am."

He heard the rustle of her skirts. She walked to the device's engine and kicked the switch. Vibrations like shock waves ran through Archie's cock. She raised the cane, and brought it down on him with deliberate, loving, cruel force. Archie jolted into the stand as he screamed and came.

Archie knelt at the countess's feet on the floor of her laboratory. His trousers were still down, but he liked the cool air on his burning bottom. It was, he felt, a most tranquil domestic scene. He lifted his head from her lap to watch her.

The countess sat in a desk chair. In one hand, she held a vial with Archie's vital fluids; in the other, a shot glass of vodka. She poured his elixir into hers. With one gulp, she drank the mixture down.

The sight made Archie's cock begin to swell again.

"Did your device allow you to see into my soul?" he asked.

"Oh, yes, Mr. Fraser." Her hand rhythmically smoothed his hair as if she were patting a lapdog. "It told me that you and I are about to embark on an adventure unlike anything you've ever experienced before. You may call on me next week, same time."

"Not sooner?"

She chuckled. "Anticipation whets the appetite." She rose

and glided to the door, leaving behind only a trace of amber and myrrh.

After he was certain she would not return. Archie came to his feet. He dressed, taking great care not to disturb the welts on his backside. He gingerly took the stairs to the foyer, where the hall porter handed him his hat.

Archie reluctantly took the steps down to the street as the door shut behind him. He glanced at the Adventurer's Club, shook his head and strode off into the London night.

INFERNAL MACHINE

Elias A. St. James

Gently, I slipped my tool into the opening, easing my way down the tight passage. I made sure to restrain myself, knowing that as eager as I was, I might damage something if I simply rushed in. Instead I moved deliberately, seeking the treasures hidden within....

"Blast!" My probe clattered to the floor as I jammed my bleeding thumb into my mouth and glared at the machine in front of me. Across the room, my lover looked up from his book.

"Elijah?" he asked, clearly wanting an explanation.

"The infernal machine savaged me," I grumbled around my thumb. I turned so that I could look at Sasha, a much more pleasant view than the obstinate machine that now seemed to be laughing at me. Aleksandr Andreyevich Koslov, affectionately called Sasha, was sprawled indolently on our bed, looking very much the dissolute Russian nobleman. I'd been dizzy in love with Aleksandr since our first day at *L'Académie des Sciences Mécaniques* in Paris. And, for some reason I never understood, he loved me in return. It couldn't have been my breeding; compared to his bloodlines, my own pedigree was pure peasantry. My father was a rabbi in a small village just outside Calais, my mother a rabbi's wife and the daughter of another rabbi. I was the oldest of six children, and until two years ago, the one destined to follow in my father's footsteps. Until the day I took apart the boiler in my mother's kitchen and redesigned it so that it was twice as efficient and used less than half the fuel. When my father saw what I had done, he decided that my younger brother would be better suited to the life of a rabbi. I, Elijah Moyse Saloman, was to be an artificer, the first ever from our village. I'd arrived in Paris without even the barest hint of the world I was going to be thrust into—wild, wicked Montmarte, with its cabarets and music halls, and its whores of either sex; and wild, wicked Sasha, whom I loved like I loved no other.

Sasha swung his legs over the edge of the bed and stood up, crossing over to sit down on the floor next to me. He was incredibly handsome, his long, dark hair hanging loose around his shoulders, his shirt hanging open to better face the heat of the summer afternoon. He frowned slightly at the machine and then poked me in the shoulder. "So what is this thing? You've not told me yet."

"I haven't?" I frowned, thinking back. Surely I'd mentioned something...?

"No. For four days you've barely said a word to me. You haven't eaten, unless I was feeding you. The only times you've come to bed was when I picked you up and put you there myself, usually after you'd passed out on the floor. So what is this thing that you are so enamored of? Other than being the most singularly ugly chair that I have ever seen?"

I grinned at his very apt description; it *was* a singularly ugly chair, if that was all it was. Surely, that was all that the iron-monger had thought it, or else he'd never have let me have it for the pittance I paid. I reached out and ran my fingers over the now-bright brass. "It's a Carstairs machine."

"It isn't!" Sasha gasped, leaning closer. "How can you tell?"

"The hinges. Look at them; no one but Carstairs used that odd box hinge." It had been that detail that had caught my eye and sent me scrambling after the cart. "That was my first hint. Then I found his mark when I was polishing the brass. There, where the seat casts a shadow. Do you see it?"

Sasha nodded, "I see it...but none of his other works are this ugly. His work was always simple and elegant."

He was right, of course. Carstairs had been the artificer's artificer, and his work had always been simple in form. The complexity, he'd always said, was on the inside. The design on this chair was elaborate, with brass scrollwork ornamenting nearly the entire construct. "An early work, do you think?" I asked.

"I don't know," Sasha shrugged. "What does it do?"

That was the question I was hoping he wouldn't ask. "I don't know yet," I admitted. "I've cleaned and polished the entire thing, I've made certain that the boiler and the tank work, I've replaced anything that looked like it might have needed to be replaced, but I can't get into this compartment." I tapped the panel that formed the pedestal for the seat. "It does open...I think. There is a seam here and hinges on the edges."

Sasha leaned in close enough that I could smell the light fragrance of the soap he used. He nodded, "I see. Well, that is annoying. You can't tell what it does without opening the case, and if you break open the case, it might not work at all." Sasha looked at me with his fabulously wicked grin. "Have you fired the boiler?"

I shook my head, "Not yet. I wanted to be certain that every-thing else worked first."

"And everything works now?"

"As far as I can tell." I glared at the recalcitrant chair. Without a word, Sasha got to his feet, fetched the pitcher from the washstand and ceremonially poured water into the tank.

"Then we shall fire this Carstairs machine and see what the master wrought and what the student rescued!" he declared, throwing an elaborate bow in my direction. I laughed and went to fetch some kindling.

It took time to get a good head of steam. When finally the gauges showed that we had adequate pressure, Sasha came to stand next to me in front of the chair to watch the show.

Nothing happened. We watched and waited in nervous silence for nearly five minutes, then Sasha coughed and looked at me.

"Is there...a switch? A lever? Some way to turn it on?" he asked.

I shook my head slowly, "Not that I found. You look. Maybe I missed it."

He knelt down and crawled around the blasted chair, hunting for a switch that I already knew didn't exist. When finally Sasha was convinced, he sat down next to me on the floor, shoulder pressing against mine, and cursed roundly in Russian before repeating himself in French.

"Four days! Four days you've wasted on this...infernally ugly chair, and all it does is clutter the room!" he railed while I sighed and turned away, starting to clean up my tools. To my surprise, Sasha grabbed the back of my shirt and pulled me into his arms, my back against his chest. "Four days where all you've done in bed is snore at me," he whispered into my ear, tugging my shirt open with one hand, his other hand slipping into my trousers and closing around my quickly hardening cock. I leaned my head back against his shoulder and was rewarded by his teeth along my neck, nibbling just hard enough to sting. He tugged at my shirt, pulling it off my shoulders, dipping his head down to lick the spot where my shoulder met my neck. Then he shifted, tipping me back until I was lying on the floor with him kneeling over me. He ran his hands down my chest to my waist, fumbling at the buttons on my trousers; I could see how his own trousers were bulging outward and moaned softly, reaching for his waist. He laughed and pushed my hands down, tugging my shirt and braces down so that my arms were tangled in them.

"Patience, *miliy moy*. You'll have that in a minute. But after four days of being driven insane by you ignoring me, I'm going to torment you a while longer." He moved down my body, tugging my trousers open and down so that my cock sprang free, then lying down on top of me, pinning me in place. He grinned down at me, his nose nearly touching mine, then kissed me hard enough that his teeth grated against mine. Sasha was taller than I and weighed nearly ten kilos more—I couldn't move him, couldn't do anything but strain and squirm under him, growing more and more aroused as he ran his agile fingers up and down my sides. He raised himself up just long enough to unbutton his own trousers and pull his cock free, then he took his place again, this time with his cock rubbing deliciously against mine.

"Sasha...please..." I whispered harshly, then yelped as he bit my neck. He started pumping his hips, his cock hot against me, growling as he worked himself into a frenzy. Dimly, I was aware of the distant sound of the bells from Saint-Pierre-de-Montmartre, the church at the top of the hill. At the sound, Sasha froze.

"No, it can't be that late," he said softly, rolling off of me and scrambling to the table. I rolled over and sat up to see him digging around in the litter on the tabletop until he found what he was looking for: his pocket watch. He opened it, looked at the time and cursed, "*Chyort voz'mi!*"

"What is it?" I asked, as I rolled over and sat up, pulling my shirt up and tucking myself back into my trousers. I could tell that our fun was over for now.

"The count is in Paris, and I'm supposed to see him tonight," Sasha answered. "I told you...oh...I told you while you were working."

I gasped in shock, "He's here? And he *wants* to see you?" I might have been one of only two people in all of Paris who actually knew the truth, who knew that while Sasha's father really was a count, his mother was not the countess. When Sasha had turned eighteen, the count had given his by-blow a handsome allowance and one-way passage to Paris, the better to hide his indiscretions. Luckily for me.

"The countess hasn't given him the son he needs. Now there's a chance that he might put her aside. In which case, he'll need an heir." Sasha hurried to the chest at the end of the bed and pulled it open, bringing out what I recognized as his best suit.

I felt my heart lurch when what he'd said sank in. "He'll bring you back to Saint Petersburg," I said softly. It was Sasha's greatest wish, I knew. He wanted to go home, and I knew that one day I'd lose him. I just hadn't expected it to be so soon.

"Not yet, I don't think," Sasha said, as he hurried through his toilette, washing up, changing his clothes, brushing his hair and then braiding it neatly. "Even if he does acknowledge me, he'll probably still want me to finish my schooling. The tsarina is said to be very fond of artificers...." He turned to look at me and must have seen something in my look, because he crossed the room and caught my face in his hands, kissing me deeply.

"I'm not leaving you, *lubov moy*," he said gently, resting his forehead against mine. He stepped back and held his arms out. "How do I look?"

I smiled at him and answered him with one of the Russian phrases he used on me, even though he often told me my accent was horrible. "*Vy ochen' krasivy.*"

"Beautiful, hm?" he repeated, laughing. "I hope the count thinks so. Keep yourself warm for me, *miliy*. I'll be back late."

"With good news, I hope."

He grinned. "Wish me luck!" He kissed me again and almost ran from the apartment, the door bouncing open as he slammed it in his haste. I followed him and closed the door, locking it behind him and turning to look at the empty apartment. Empty except for a bed and clothes press, a rickety table, bookcases made from pieces of packing crates and bricks, and, of course, the most singularly ugly chair in France. Our only chair, really, since Sasha and I had broken our only other chair a week before.

I sighed and tugged my shirt off, throwing it onto the bed with a muttered curse. There was nothing I could do about Sasha; by the time he came back, he'd be a nobleman in truth, and from tonight on, he'd be counting the days until he returned to Saint Petersburg. And I'd be counting the days until he left me behind. After all, what could a rabbi's son offer a count?

There was nothing I could do about that infernal machine, either. Apparently, all it was good for was, as Sasha had so aptly put it, cluttering up our room. Although... I gave it a long look and then turned to the shelf where we kept a bottle of oil. Perhaps that chair would be good for something, after all.

It was a strange affectation of mine, and one that Sasha often teased me about, but I disliked masturbating on our bed. It somehow felt dishonest. I stripped off my trousers and poured some oil into my hand, slowly smoothing it over my still-hard cock. Prepared, I sat down on the chair, finding the ugly thing oddly comfortable. I wrapped my hand around my cock and closed my eyes, thinking about Sasha, the smell of his skin, the feel of his hands on me and his cock against mine; the way he loved to tease me until I couldn't stand or speak; the way his mouth felt on my mouth, on my cock.... I moaned softly and leaned back a little in the chair, my back pressing against the cool metal. Without warning, the back shifted. The seat sank, just enough to notice. I heard something click, and gears began to turn.

I had done my work well. Before I could gather my thoughts, the mechanism was working, and the ornate scrollwork snapped to life like a trap, pinning my arms to my sides, catching both of my legs, caging my head so that I couldn't turn. I struggled, unable to move at all as the gears kept on turning. The panel that I'd been so desperate to get into earlier opened, the sides rising and taking my legs with them, spreading them wide until it felt like my hips were going to snap. By the time the movement stopped, the chair had tipped back so I was helplessly reclined. I tested my bonds and cursed—I was stuck and likely to stay that way until Sasha returned and could figure out how to release me. Then I heard another click, and the gears began to turn once more. That was when I saw movement; a pair of metal arms appeared, one rising from between my legs, the other dropping from over my head, and I caught my breath in wonder as I saw what embellished the end of each arm.

The artificer in me saw first that they were beautifully made wooden cocks on the arms with the finest articulation that I had ever seen. That voice was quickly silenced when one of the cocks stopped at a level with my hips, and the other lowered itself toward the cage that imprisoned my head. A cage, I suddenly noticed, that had an opening over the mouth that was just large enough to admit the wooden intruder now approaching.

"No..." I whispered. "No! Stop!" I twisted as much as I could, all the while ordering the machine to stop, to release me. It didn't accept voice commands, and soon I wasn't in any position to give them anymore. It actually wasn't unpleasant—the cock wasn't too large, and the wood was smooth and warm. I ran my tongue over the surface, finding myself growing aroused again. As if it could tell what I was feeling, the movement of the arm paused for a moment, then slowly started to pump, fucking my mouth gently.

The cock in my mouth muffled my shout of surprise at the sudden pressure against my ass. That cock slid in smoothly, as if it had been greased, and started moving in a slow, steady rhythm that left me moaning and wanting more. I could feel the sweat making my skin slick under the metal bonds, allowing me to shift just enough to emphasize how completely I was bound. This wasn't my first experience with being bound for sex; Sasha had discovered a taste for it somewhere and had taught me. Sasha insisted that we take turns, but I much preferred being bound, and the tighter the bonds, the better I liked it. It was, in truth, the way that we had broken our chair the week before.

The speed of the pumping increased, and I closed my eyes, sucking hard on the cock in my mouth, imagining that it was Sasha fucking my mouth, his cock in my ass, pounding harder and faster, making me strain against the straps as I tried to move with him, pull him deeper, silently begging him to make me scream. My orgasm was building, harder than ever before. Perhaps that was why it took several minutes for me to notice that the machine had stopped moving, and even longer to gather my wits and understand what had happened.

In the end, the answer was ridiculously simple—Sasha had

only put enough water in the tank to test the mechanism. I groaned in frustration and waited for the machine to release me. Only there was no slacking of the straps, no movement, no release. After several long minutes, I realized that the straps weren't going to move, that the empty tanks meant that I'd be stuck until Sasha came home.

If he ever did. I whimpered as the nasty little thought occurred to me. Suppose the count didn't want Sasha to finish his schooling? Suppose he wanted his new heir to return to Saint Petersburg with him immediately? What then? He wouldn't need his books any more, and any clothes he had here would never be suitable for the heir to a count. There would be no reason for Sasha to come back to the apartment. No reason at all.

Panic struck all at once, grabbing me in its fist and squeezing. He was gone, he was never coming back, I was trapped and I would die like this. I screamed and fought the straps, lost in primal terror until at last I passed out from exhaustion, falling into a restless sleep punctuated with vague, terror-filled dreams.

I woke to the rattle of a key in the lock and the groaning of the door hinges. In the faint moonlight, I could see Sasha coming into the apartment and almost wept with relief. He closed the door quietly, no doubt thinking me asleep. As soon as the door closed, I started to grunt, struggling weakly and trying to get his attention. I heard his breath catch.

"*Illyusha?*" he called softly, sounding confused. I heard the floor creak as he moved, then the lamp flared and the room filled with dim light. I could see him frowning at the empty bed. Then he turned a little more and faced me. His eyes went wide, "*Bozhe moi!*"

It wasn't hard to know what he was seeing: his lover, bound in brass, obscenely spread and presented like a two-franc whore, impaled by a pair of wooden cocks. I grunted again, and Sasha startled, rushing forward and stopping at my side, his hands hovering over my torso.

"*Illyusha*, are you all right?" he asked, his eyes darting here and there, taking in all the information he could. He grabbed the gag and tried to pull it from my mouth; it didn't move. I grunted, and he met my eyes and grimaced. "Once for yes, twice for no."

I grunted once, and he relaxed. Then he scowled, "There's no way for you to tell me what happened. Or how to get you out of this."

I closed my eyes for a moment, then did my best to say the word 'water' around the gag. He looked puzzled, then shook his head.

"Lets stay with yes and no. Ah...you found how to turn it on? No? Then this was an accident. I see." He walked around behind the chair, and I heard him moving there. "The boiler is cold...*Illyusha*, you've been like this for hours?"

I grunted once, and he reappeared, "*Miliy*, do I need to get a sledge?"

I grunted twice, emphatically, and he held his hands up, "All right! No smashing the machine. But I do need to get you out of there." He glared at the chair, crouching down. Then he stood up and ran his fingers through his hair. "I don't know. Let me... let me fire the boiler. Perhaps that will make it start doing..." He gestured and stepped back, shaking his head. "I'll fill the tank to the top this time."

It took him five trips to the cistern and then an impossibly long time crouched out of sight. Finally, he reappeared.

"It will take some time for the pressure to build enough for the mechanism to work," he said, resting one hand on my stomach. "So, shall I guess what happened?"

I grunted, and he smiled slowly, "You were being impatient, weren't you?" His fingers started to trail over my skin, skipping over the brass straps, fluttering over my nipples until I groaned. He laughed and pulled away, "So impatient. You couldn't have waited for me? Now, should I let you wait? Let this amazing discovery of yours finish you off?" He smiled at me and crossed his arms over his chest, "Or shall I entertain myself while we wait? Because you really do look very inviting like this."

Just the idea of Sasha touching me, doing whatever he willed while I was helplessly bound by Carstairs's infernal chair was enough to make me moan in lust, make my cock slowly start to rise again. He laughed and moved to stand between my legs.

"I assume that is a yes?" he asked. Without waiting for my answering grunt, he grabbed my half-hard cock in his hand and slowly started to stroke me erect. He knew what I liked, what sent me off like a Roman candle. And he knew very well how to keep me on the edge, keep me growing ever more frantic until at last he allowed me release. That is what he proceeded to do to me, playing with my cock and bollocks, licking my nipples with his rough tongue, then biting them hard enough to make me yell around the gag. He tried tugging on the cock buried in my ass and found that he could get enough movement to make me gasp and moan. Then he grinned wickedly at me and proceeded to strip away his own clothing, letting the pieces fall where they would until he was naked, his erection standing out proudly. He studied me for a long moment, then stepped back, a satisfied look on his face.

"Oh, this will be interesting," he said. He turned away and picked up the bottle of oil, pouring a liberal amount into his palm. Then he moved to stand next to me, dousing my cock with the oil, anointing it like some pagan icon until it shone in the dim light. Without any hesitation, he climbed up to straddle me, my cock pressing against his ass. His eyes twinkled as he looked down at me and said, "Why should you have all the fun, hm?"

He lowered himself slowly, and as he did so, I heard the gears start to turn again, and the cock in my ass started to move once more. I squeaked around the gag, and Sasha stopped moving, looking at me and seeing the cock fucking my mouth.

"*Bozhe moi...*" he murmured, his breath coming faster as he took me into himself, surrounding me with heat and delicious pressure. When he could go no farther, when I was as deep as I ever had been, he started to rock, one hand resting on my abdomen as he used his oil-slick hand to stroke his own cock. I could hear Sasha's moans of pleasure over the music of the machine, feel his body growing tighter around me, and I knew that he would shoot before too long. The cock in my ass picked that moment to pick up speed, pumping harder and faster than Sasha ever could. The cock in my mouth plunged deeper into my throat, cutting off the muffled sounds of my screams of pleasure as I shot. A moment later, I felt warm wet splattering on my chest, and Sasha slumped over me, breathing heavily.

He raised his head and looked at me. "I wish I could kiss you."

I grunted once, tired and sore and wondering what would happen next. I could hear the gears turning still, even though the cocks had fallen quiet. Then the chair shuddered; Sasha looked alarmed and scrambled off of my lap, looking at me warily.

He need not have been so alarmed. I felt the cocks sliding from my mouth and ass, then the chair shuddered and straightened, the straps receding until they once again resembled nothing more than scrollwork on a singularly ugly chair. I stayed where I was, my head resting against the back of the chair, completely spent.

"*Illyusha?*" Sasha said quietly. "Can you move?"

I swallowed, feeling the soreness in my throat. "I don't know."

"Give me your hand." Sasha took my hand and tugged me to my feet, then caught me when my poor, abused legs gave out and I tumbled to the floor. We sprawled together for a moment, then he kissed me, deep and slow.

The kiss was interrupted by a long *wheesh* sound from the chair; we both jumped and turned to see steam escaping through the seams in the pedestal.

"It cleans itself," Sasha murmured, wonder in his voice. "Is there anything that Carstairs didn't think of?"

"A safety release," I answered wryly, drawing a laugh from Sasha. I looked up at him and smiled. "Thank you for coming back," I whispered.

He looked puzzled. "Where else would I go?"

Reluctantly, I told him of my panic; he drew me into his arms and held me tightly.

"*Miliy moy*, I'd no more leave you behind than I'd fly to the moon. I made it very clear to my father...oh, yes, he's acknowledged me! I told him that I would marry to suit my station, but that you were going to be at my side for the rest of my days." He sobered. "If...if that's what you want. Is that what you want, *Illyusha?*"

I blinked, almost too tired to understand what he was saying, "You want me to come to Saint Petersburg with you?"

"Yes, if you're willing."

"I..." I couldn't think. All I could do was pull his head down to mine and kiss him. He smiled against my lips.

"I assume that is a yes?" he whispered.

"After all," I murmured back. "The tsarina is said to be fond of artificers."

"And I'll be bringing the genius who rebuilt a Carstairs

machine into her court," he added. He looked past me at the now-quiescent chair, and a slow smile spread across his face. He looked back at me. "My turn?"

"Oh, yes!"

DOCTOR WATSON MAKES A HOUSE CALL

Essemoh Teepee

D amn it, cabby can't you stoke it harder?" Watson called out through the open window. Any reply was drowned out by the noise of steam hissing and six iron legs beating a drumroll on the road.

The London train from Liverpool Street Station had been delayed. Watson had engaged a fast steam carriage from Bishop Stortford to his destination at Dunmow, hoping to make up the time. The Steam Steed hissed and clattered along the Essex Lane to Easton Lodge, the Countess of Warwick's country house, as fast as its articulated legs would take it. Watson feared he was still going to be late. He sat in the cab behind the steam engine bouncing along the deeply rutted lane and held on to his bags. A brass-bound wooden box on the floor he trapped with his boot so it could not move around. It would not do to arrive not only late but with his equipment unusable.

The invitation had come in to 221b Baker Street for Mr. Sherlock Holmes and Dr. John Watson. The Count and Countess of

Warwick requested the pleasure of Mr. Holmes's company and also had need of Dr. Watson in a consulting capacity. Holmes had dismissed the invitation,

"They want me to perform at the dinner table, and you to demonstrate your toys in the bedchambers, Watson. You go if you wish; I do not feel like being a curiosity for the gentry."

Watson had a living to earn and the Countess of Warwick's society house parties were famous. A previous case, that of the unfortunate Lady Annabella King née Lovelace's empty box, had crossed Lady Daisy Greville's path with that of Holmes.

Watson had acquired something very special from Lady Annabella. She had scribbled a will before leaving the doctor tied to her bed and making her escape from his protection. Annabella must have known that Professor Moriarty would betray her. Knowing that she was probably going to her death, she had still gone in the hope of saving her lost husband. Watson looked at the box on the floor. The unique contents were fast making him his fortune in the months since that fateful day.

Watson thought back to his studies of hysterical paroxysm with the great Jean-Martin Charcot at the Salpêtrière Hospital in Paris. The long days learning particular massage techniques had been hard. He smiled recalling the even longer Parisian nights.

Meeting Holmes on his return to England had been fortunate. Sharing rooms at Baker Street had helped him get on his feet until his practice had picked up. Commissions from troubled women and their long-suffering husbands were now steady and lucrative. However, what was in the box was singular in his field and much in demand by those who knew of its existence.

Watson enjoyed his work. He could not agree with some colleagues that the treatments for female hysteria were time consuming and tricky. He felt that if he could bring his patients a release from the grip of their affliction, then his ministrations were a satisfaction in themselves. That the fees were fat and readily paid was a matter of concern for no one else.

Easton Lodge was very grand. Watson stood on the gravel drive surrounded by his bags and the box. Looking up at its ivy-covered façade, he felt a sense of history, Empire and money. The noise of the Steam Steed hissing and clanking away brought the butler to the big oak doors.

"Dr. Watson? The Countess is expecting you." The butler sounded huffy as he took one of Watson's bags. "She has been waiting in the private drawing room."

"My train was unavoidably delayed," Watson explained, only to receive a rude sound in response. *Not a good beginning,* Watson thought.

"Dr. Watson, your Ladyship. He said his train was delayed." The unpleasant butler sounded quite disbelieving.

"Thank you, William, that will be all. I will ring if we require anything. See to it that we are not disturbed." Watson thought that Lady Daisy Greville, Countess of Warwick, looked a trifle flushed and her voice sounded a little strained. He swore he heard the butler make another rude noise as he shut the door behind him.

"Mr. Sherlock Holmes sends his regrets my Lady; he is otherwise engaged on a case at present and was unable to accompany me," Watson lied.

"Never matter Doctor; Bertie is not too happy with him in any case after the unfortunate events around Mr. Holmes's last visit to this house. It was my husband's idea to invite Mr. Holmes; it was I who invited you," Lady Daisy said.

"The Prince of Wales is here, my Lady?" Unlike Holmes, Watson had only ever seen the Prince from afar and he was curious to meet him. Watson knew, like most of society, that the

Prince and the Countess were closely acquainted.

"Dear Bertie leaves later today; he is to be in Brighton tonight. The Palace is sending a dirigible for him." Lady Daisy patted the chaise lounge and went on, "Come and sit beside me, Doctor, I want you to tell me how you knew poor dear Annabella. We were such good friends and I was surprised that she left you her, her device. She had told me all about it. The poor woman left me some of her books."

Watson saw that the Countess had been looking through a copy of Gilles de la Tourette's remarkable line drawings of women in paroxysm. The three volumes of photographs of the same subject matter by Desire Magloire Bourneville were on a side table.

Watson thought Lady Daisy's cheeks if anything looked even brighter. The tip of her delicate pink tongue kept moistening her lips. He diagnosed that the Countess was greatly in need of his particular skills, not a cosy chat. He took her hand and felt it clammy in his; her pulse under his fingers was racing.

"My dear Lady, you are discomfited, how may I be of help to you in your distress?" Watson knew perfectly well what the Countess needed, but there were niceties and protocols to be observed.

"I am all of a fluster, Doctor; perhaps if you were to examine me you could give an opinion as to my ailment?" Daisy looked into Watsons eyes and a slight smile trembled on her lips.

"But of course, my Lady. Your skirts, if you would be so kind?" Watson watched as with some alacrity the Countess leant and gathered her white frilly skirts and full petticoat in her hands and drew them above her waist. She was wearing white lacy stockings with her patent pumps. Red satin ribbons around the tops of her thighs held up her stockings; she was not wearing any bloomers.

The Countess' skin was alabaster white and the fine red curls on her pubis looked downy soft. Watson realized that he was holding his breath and tried to appear detached and professional. Her perfume and the musk rising from her clearly wet sex were exquisite; he felt his cock swelling against the front of his pants. Swallowing with some difficulty, he said, "A little wider if you will, my Lady."

Daisy spread her legs for Watson and leant back against the silk cushions. He thought he heard her sigh and saw that her eyes were closed. She was warm and soft to his touch, her labia slick with secretions that confirmed his initial thoughts. Lady Daisy was indeed in great distress. His forefinger slid readily into her sex. A low moan escaped her slightly parted lips as he explored her internally. The Countess was very wet but still quite tight. Watson decided that he would work her with his hand first before applying any instruments.

Two fingers required a little twisting and easing before they could enter her fully. Daisy kept moving her hips slowly as though trying to press against his fist. He was surprised at her seeming maidenly appearance. According to all the society tales Daisy Greville, Countess of Warwick, was not inexperienced in matters of the bedchamber. Watson considered that perhaps this was part of her charms. Along with her beauty and sharp wit she was like a fresh young girl in bed. He wondered if the Prince of Wales liked his women to be tight.

His examination found the sensitive area of her vaginal walls that lay at the base of her clitoris. His experiences in Paris had shown him that firm massage here had great efficacy. Daisy's gasps and whimpers attested to his successful application of that knowledge. He worked his fingers in her harder and faster.

"Oh, dear Doctor, I am about to faint!" the Countess cried out.

"Allow yourself the release, my Lady." Watson said quietly and she curled up around his penetrating hand, shuddering and sobbing in spasm. Watson slowly reduced the pressure of his fingers and gradually slid them out of her.

A few moments later she opened her eyes and smiled up at him saying, "Oh, my word, Doctor, you are very good indeed. What else do you have that will ease my dreadful distress? Do tell, what is in the box?"

Watson smiled and reached for the bag carried by the butler.

"This device will help maintain a degree of stimuli my Lady, while I prepare. You apply it just here and squeeze this like so." Watson guided Daisy's fingers and showed her how to make the small hand vibrator buzz against her clitoris.

"Oh, my! That feels most unusual, Doctor. Press just here you say?" Daisy asked.

"Quite so, my Lady." Watson busied himself unpacking the box and setting up while the Countess rubbed and vibrated herself to several more paroxysms. He saw that her labia were now quite red and swollen. The vibrator was making wet sounds as she eased it in and out of her opening and he judged her ready for the next stage of treatment.

"I am ready, my Lady," Watson said, and he saw Daisy's eyes open very wide as she looked at the engine clamped to a side table. Watson had maneuvered the table so that it was in front of her hips.

"Is that Annabella's 'Vibrador,' Doctor? It looks quite fearsome." Daisy raised her eyebrows at Watson.

"A Vibrador-a-vapor-cura-histeria, my Lady. The Lady Annabella had it modified to use the Faraday-Babbage fireless steam motor. This small brass ball is a tireless steam engine that drives the piston here." Watson pointed out the elements of the device to the Countess.

"Will all of that go into me, Doctor?" Daisy indicated the thick, realistically sculpted phallus attached to the piston rod.

"I judge that you are in a condition ready to accommodate this particular size, my Lady. It will have a considerable effect on your affliction," Watson explained.

"I am sure it will, my good Doctor, I am sure it will," The Countess murmured as she lay back once more. She hooked one thigh over the armrest and spread her other leg along the couch, opening herself very wide. "I am ready, Doctor."

Watson coated the head of the phallus with a little lubricating ointment and eased the round head between Daisy's labia. Her gasp as it stretched her entry was as he expected. He noted with satisfaction the involuntary rising of her hips to aid the penetration.

"I shall begin on a low setting, my Lady and we will see how you progress," Watson explained and twisted a lever. The piston slowly extended from the mechanism and the phallus slid deeper into the Countess. Her moan became a soft whimper as the piston began to cycle slowly. The metal rod thrust the dildo in and out in a steadily increasing rhythm.

"That is so very satisfactory, Doctor; a little faster perhaps?" Daisy sighed.

"Of course, my Lady," Watson said, adjusting the mechanism to speed up the thrusting and increase the depth of penetration.

"Just there, good Doctor, just there. Ohh!" Daisy arched her back and pushed her hips onto the impaling phallus in time with its cycle. The vision of the shaft slipping between her spread labia, glistening with her natural lubrication, caused Watson's cock to ache unbearably. He judged that her paroxysms would begin soon.

"Oh, my god, Doctor. I am undone!" Daisy cried out and

began shuddering repeatedly. Tears were squeezing from under her tightly closed eyelids. Watson allowed the Vibrador to massage the Countess for some minutes more as she repeatedly cried out and ground her hips around the thrusting piston. His hand furtively squeezed his stiffness through the cloth of his pants. No, Watson very definitely did not consider these treatments to be a time-consuming chore.

"Come here, Doctor! I need your comfort!" Daisy reached for him as he approached. This too was not unusual in Watson's experience; in many regards it was to be hoped for. He often found it calmed his patients even more to feel him intimately close.

The Countess's fingers fumbled at the buttons of his fly and he had to help her undo his pants. She grasped his erection in a firm grip and drew him closer. It was Watson's turn to moan as he felt her soft lips engulf his penis and suck him into her hot mouth. He always allowed his patients to control the depth and speed of the fellatio; that way it was more proper he thought.

Daisy was very skilled in the erotic practice, confirming Watson's opinion of her attraction as a paramour to powerful men. Watson wondered what the Prince of Wales would think about sharing his mistress's mouth with a mere consulting doctor. Then he had no thoughts other than the tension between his legs and Daisy's hand stroking his testicles as she sucked on his glans. He was close to ejaculation and thought it best to say so.

"My Lady, I am about to spend!"

Daisy sucked on his cock all the harder and swallowed his shaft to the very back of her throat. He felt her sweet nose crushed against his pubic hair. Then he spurted his semen down her throat with a deep growl in his own. The Countess seemed to take no small pleasure in sucking every drop of his seed and licking him clean.

The machine was still pounding her, making wet sucking sounds. The Countess's hips were riding the shaft with some determination. Watson reached down and fingered her damp curls. He found the slippery pearl of her clitoris and rubbed it hard with two fingers. Daisy flung her arms wide and her head back at his expert touch. Her voice rose higher and higher in a keening cry that ended in a yelp as he pinched his thumb and finger together. The Countess gave a small scream as she convulsed on the chaise lounge. She fell back in a seeming swoon and Watson hurriedly went to still the machine.

Luncheon was served on the terrace under white canvas awnings. White linen tablecloths dazzled the eye under gleaming Irish crystal glassware and antique silver cutlery. Equally glittering houseguests thronged the tables consuming the gourmet fare with near gluttonous gusto. Doctor Watson ate quietly, watching the interactions of the social elite. He was fascinated by the presence of the overweight figure of the Prince of Wales at the head of the table. The women guests hung on his every word and all laughed uproariously at his slightest bon mot. There had been a brief introduction to His Royal Highness before lunch.

"Dashed shame about that Babbage woman and her box of secrets, Doctor. Your Mr. Holmes should have been a sight more careful of that Faraday Babbage thing if you ask me," the Prince had said.

"It was very sad, Your Highness, that the Lady Annabella was so brutally murdered by Moriarty's henchmen," Watson had replied.

"Quite so, quite so I'm sure. If we only had her damned secret of fireless steam we might've stumped cousin Willhelm. Mama doesn't think he's a threat, d'you know; she won't be told." The Prince spoke more to himself than Watson.

"I am sure that the Queen will do what she thinks is right for the Empire, Sir," Watson said as diplomatically as he could. but the Prince had already begun walking off toward the tables.

Watson thought of Holmes and his misgivings over the secret of the little brass ball falling into anyone's hands. The doctor trusted that his friend knew best in such things. The destruction of the secret was probably for the best. He still had the little ball with its impenetrable formula and at least it was doing some good in his hands. The doctor noted that the Countess seemed much calmer now, with almost a glow about her complexion. She was in very animated conversation with a woman who kept glancing down the table toward Watson.

The meal came to a sudden end when a hissing clatter in the sky grew ever louder. The houseguests rose in a group to see the arrival of the Royal dirigible. The huge red and gold torpedo sailed slowly through the sky trailing smoke from its high-pressure steam aeroboilers. Fine coal dust blown into the furnaces superheated the steam driving the spinning aerovanes. Watson loved dirigible travel as much as Holmes hated it. The doctor thought it had more to do with the incident over Paris than any fear of heights.

The Prince and his equerry climbed aboard to whistles and salutes from the Airnavy crew clinging to the rigging.

"Impressive sight, what?" a guest said to Watson. "Makes one proud of Empire, what?"

"Yes, I suppose it must," Watson replied as they watched the airship rise into the air again. It slowly spun on its center line and turned its prow toward the south. Thick smoke poured out as it moved away ever faster. The Prince would be on time for dinner in the Pavilion, the grand folly a previous prince had created to impress his mistress. *Nothing changes,* Watson thought.

Watson spied the Countess talking animatedly with a group

of the ladies who had been paying court to the Prince at lunch. Some of them kept looking in his direction and covering their faces coyly with their hands. He sighed when the Countess took the hands of two expensively dressed women and drew them in his direction.

"Doctor Watson, these are my two most dear, closest friends. I have told them all about you and they want to consult with you, in private." Daisy Greville, Countess of Warwick, gently ushered the two blushing, giggling women toward Doctor Watson.

"Of course my Lady, it will be my pleasure to attend to their every need," Watson said. *It is going to be a busy afternoon and likely the night also,* he thought to himself as the four of them made their way indoors.

THE TREATMENT

D. L. King

tell you, Harold, the woman is pure evil. You know they call her the dragon lady, don't you?"

"Rufus, please. Aren't you being just a tad overdramatic? After all, you claim any woman who manages to excite your—baser instincts—is 'evil.' Don't you think that's a bit old-fashioned?"

"Harold, the clothing she wears..."

"Is stunning!"

"But the way she flaunts her body. Why, it's as if she, and please forgive my saying it, were—naked! She wears no corset. In fact, I'd imagine she wears no foundation garments at all. How could she, in clothing so shockingly skin tight? Why it's simply shameful. My god, man, you can see every curve of her form—every curve."

A few heads turned toward them.

"It seems you've given the matter a great deal of thought, Rufus, old man."

Generally, members of the club took great pains to give at least the impression of privacy. Though it seemed, when it came to the female form, no man's utter discretion could be counted upon. There was some general harrumphing before the butler brought fresh whiskey and whispered, "Gentlemen, please!" As the two men's voices lowered, heads turned back to perusing copies of the *Times* or feigning interest in more polite conversation again.

"Oh, really Rufus," Harold whispered, "she is a Chinese, after all. She merely wears the clothing of her custom. Don't be such a prig."

"It is not, I tell you. I've checked and other Orientals wear a loose-fitting affair, certainly just as shameful, but not nearly so revealing. It's her, I tell you; she's planning something nefarious, mark my words."

"I'm joining her for tea this afternoon. Why don't you come along and let me formally introduce you. I'm sure once you've met her you'll feel differently."

The young man shed his clothing and handed each item he removed to the maid standing before him. Once completely naked, he followed her into the cavernous room and waited while she fastened the leather belt and wrist and ankle cuffs. He climbed into what he'd come to think of as his own special pod and allowed the maid to place smoked goggles over his eyes and a bit, made of rubber, into his mouth. He felt his cock rising even as he was being tied down. All this was for his own good, he reminded himself. It was a sacrifice he made for his health and vigor, otherwise he'd never let himself be subjected to Miss Li's treatment.

Li Mei sat writing at her secretary:

* * *

It is as I assumed. The young Englishman has an extraordinary amount of untapped energy, waiting to be harvested. Due to societal propriety and his acceptance that the female of the species is to be cosseted and revered, most of the young men of the upper and upper middle classes have very little experience of the flesh, other than as practiced alone, furtively, under their bedclothes, in the dark of night. It must be noted, however, that males between the ages of eighteen and twenty-two provide the best possibilities, as much older and their social conditioning begins to tarnish as does their overabundance of energy. I must, however, note that the above premise does not hold true for young men of the ruling class, as they have been taught that all pleasure is their birthright, as long as privacy is maintained. They are, therefore, not nearly the abundant source of energy as are their brothers of a slightly lower status.

The light on the desk flickered.

"Gentlemen to see you, Miss Li." Mei's maid proffered two calling cards on a silver tray.

"Ah, Harold. And he's brought a little friend with him, how perfectly lovely. Show them out to the garden. After they've been settled, go upstairs and help Gabrielle with the machine." She looked toward the lamp on her desk. "We seem to be experiencing a power drain."

Mei adjusted the red and gold lacquer chopsticks holding her black hair in a tight chignon. She applied just a bit more rouge to her lips, but nothing else. Her porcelain skin and dark eyes needed no embellishment other than the pinch of a cheek to add the hint of rose.

Her black and red dress had dragons woven into the silk in

golden thread. She had adapted the design of the dress from some of the newer styles she'd seen in China, but she had gone much further than was even the least bit proper. The style really was quite shocking. It had a high collar, split in the middle, and long fitted sleeves. The dress hugged her breasts and cinched in naturally at her waist. The hemline came only to midcalf, showing the loose, black silk trousers she wore underneath. Both sides of the formfitting skirt were slit from hem to knee, making it easier to move. Her current experiment called for the charming and seduction of young men, and the style of her dress helped immensely.

"Harold, so good of you to come. And who is this charming young fellow with you?"

Both men rose when Mei approached the table. Rufus's eyes went wide as she sat and he turned to Harold. "You see, there are dragons on her attire," he whispered.

"Ah, you're commenting on the design of the silk? I was born in the year of the dragon and so I have a natural affinity to their form. Are you a fan of dragons Mr....?"

"I'm terribly sorry, my dear Miss Li; this is my friend, Rufus Hamilton. I hope you don't mind I've brought him?"

"Ma'am," Rufus said, with a slight tilt of his head.

"Not at all. I'm very happy to make your acquaintance. Please, Mr. Hamilton, take your seat. The dragon, it is said, is the mightiest of the birth signs. Dragon people are quite an independent lot, but we enjoy the spectacle of a good party. Are you a believer in astrology, Mr. Hamilton? I'm more a believer in science, but I am attracted to the artistic representation of my birth sign.

"Ah, here's the tea. I do hope you enjoy it. It's my own special blend of jasmine and black teas and the cakes are a special Chinese pastry. I make them myself." The maid set the tray down and Li Mei poured.

"What an interesting flavor. I don't believe I've tasted anything quite like it. And Rufus, these sweets are simply astonishing. You must try one. I've no idea what's in them but they're delicious," Harold said.

The maid cleared her throat and whispered something, in Chinese, to Mei, who stood, followed immediately by the young men. "Please, sirs, sit. There is some small household emergency to which I must attend. I'll shan't be gone long, I promise. Until then, please enjoy your tea."

The machine occupied most of the third floor of the house. When Mei arrived there was quite a bit of commotion. A naked young man thrashed about in a web of black rubber hoses and silk cords while two maids stood by helplessly. Mei shut and bolted the heavy door behind her.

"For heaven's sake, Freddie, what on earth is the problem?" The man made little grunting noises behind a rubber bit in his mouth. Mei kissed his forehead and he calmed slightly. She removed his goggles and his eyes pleaded with her.

She scanned the metal monstrosity and saw steam escaping from one of the pipes about fifty feet from where she stood, and she recognized the problem immediately. The leak was causing the machine to malfunction. It had slowed the action of the pump, which had most likely created some uncomfortable friction with Freddie's anal insert, as well as a disturbing change in the pressure on his nipples and testicles. Oh, poor Freddie.

"Freddie, darling, I think it's time you thought about going home, don't you? I'll just bring you some tea to refresh you. Then you may get dressed and be on your way. She unfastened a rubber strap around his head and removed the black rubber bit in his mouth.

Stretching his jaw, he said, "Yes, Miss Li. It's just I feel so tired now, I have hardly any strength left... But I know the treatments are still working."

"Well, it's no wonder, the way you were thrashing about; of course you're tired."

"I woke and you were gone and things were starting to pinch and all. I'm sorry about the trouble—but with the pinching and the rubbing... You will let me return, though, won't you?"

"Of course, dear Freddie. And I'm so sorry about the discomfort you experienced; completely my fault. It shall be fixed at once."

"Well, then, perhaps I should stay a bit longer..."

"No, Freddie. You've been here most of the day. It's time for you to go home and rest; recover your strength. You may return next Saturday for another treatment. As always, I must caution you against the dangers of self-abuse between now and then. After all, that is why you've come for treatment, isn't it?"

"Yes, ma'am."

"You're such a good boy, Freddie. Gabrielle will help you out of the machine and get you dressed and on your way."

Mei pulled Gabrielle aside. "Quickly, as soon as he's gone, bind and seal that leak, then stoke the furnace and get the pressure back up to capacity. I've two new boys in the garden right now! I want the machine back up and running within the hour. Drat, what a waste of a day. Now the electrical current in the house is almost depleted and we were unable to harvest any new electricity from the machine's manipulation of Freddie."

Rufus and Harold were much more relaxed by the time Mei returned to the garden. The opiates in the tea and cakes had served to loosen up their normally ridged sense of decorum. They'd taken off their jackets and undone their collars and were enjoying the unusually sunny afternoon.

Stepping between them, Mei put a hand on each man's shoulder, letting it slide down his chest until she found his nipple underneath the shirt. Lightly caressing them both, she said, "Since arriving in England, I've been pondering something. I hope you two might shed some light on the subject. Please, give me your honest opinion. Do you think this style of dress is too immodest?"

They turned toward her to look as she ran her hands down the sides of her breasts, over her waist and ended in a resting position, index fingers and thumbs touching, framing the area where her mound of Venus lay beneath the layers of silk. Harold giggled uncontrollably, but Rufus just stared at her hands.

"Why, Mr. Hamilton, you must have eaten quite a lot of cake. Look how tight your trousers have become. Are they terribly uncomfortable?"

Eyes remaining on the prize, Rufus nodded his head in the affirmative.

"And dear Mr. Martin," she went on, as Harold made an effort to stop giggling, "it looks as though your pants could do with some alteration, as well." She moved her hands up, over her flat stomach, to frame her breasts, and noticed the motion was not lost on either young man. Mouths dropped open as they followed her every movement. "Gentlemen, won't you join me in the library?"

Once Rufus and Harold were made comfortable in matching wing chairs, the maid served more tea. "Rufus, dear, do you think you might like to unbutton your trousers? They seem so uncomfortably tight. I'm sure it would put you much more at your ease." Rufus's hands automatically went to open his pants as Mei urged him on. "There, that's better, isn't it?" She noted his spectacular erection and thanked her good fortune that Harold had decided to bring his friend along. "You, too,

Harold. You wouldn't want your friend to be on his own, would you?" Mei watched as Harold opened his pants. Though his tumescence was still building, Mei doubted it would be quite as grand as his friend's, but it would be perfectly adequate.

"Young men today seem to have a dangerous buildup of excess energy. It isn't good for your chi to have such an over-abundance of energy. It makes you think unclean thoughts. Sometimes it even makes you—abuse yourself. Have either of you experienced such unwanted thoughts or perhaps even been driven to touch and fondle yourself impurely?"

Both men's hands went directly to their genitals. Harold slid his foreskin over and back, over and back, seemingly uncon-sciously, while Rufus buried his fist between his legs and kneaded his testicles. They gazed upon Mei with rapt attention.

"I can help you with this problem. Help rid you of this unwanted energy so that your chi is your own once again."

Rufus took another drink from his teacup. "Miss Li?"

"Yes, Rufus?"

"What is 'chi,' please?"

"Why, it is nothing less than your life force, Rufus. You see how very important this is? It is your very life force of which I speak."

"Oh, I see, well, yes. That is important, then."

"Now, wouldn't you like me to help you with your problem? I can promise you a very pleasurable treatment, after which you will return home feeling much more confi-dent about your personal deportment." Mei stepped between the two men and gently wrapped her hands around their fully engorged penises and squeezed. They looked at her with such grateful eyes, while her own thoughts turned to the amount of palpable electromagnetic potential in the room. "Now, come with me and I shall introduce you to some most inscrutable

Oriental wisdom. I promise you'll leave my home new men."

Mei led Harold and Rufus upstairs to the third floor and a small anteroom before the machine room. "You must remove all your clothing before entering the treatment area."

"But surely you must be joking, Miss Lee," Rufus exclaimed. Harold had already begun to unbutton his shirt. "You can't expect us to be—naked—in front of you. It would be unseemly."

The effects of the tea seemed to be wearing off. Mei thought quickly. "If you were ill and visiting a physician who asked you to remove your clothing, I'm sure you wouldn't hesitate, would you?"

"No, but..."

"In this instance, and for this purpose, you must think of me as your own personal physician. I am, after all, trained to treat your particular chi problem and have done so with many other young men. You mustn't think of me as a beautiful woman but as a practitioner of the physical arts. If you would feel more comfortable, I'll wait for you inside the treatment room and Ting and Gabrielle can help you both undress. Gabrielle, please fetch more tea for our young friends."

"Yes, well, I think that would be best," Rufus said. Harold had finished unbuttoning his shirt but was having a difficult time removing it, as he hadn't unfastened the cuff links. Ting helped him off with the shirt and hung it in a closet as Gabrielle came back with two cups of tea.

"Drink your tea, Mr. Hamilton," Mei prompted. "It will help to settle your nerves. You, as well, Harold. Now I'll just await you inside."

Once the maids had helped them off with their clothing, Rufus and Harold were escorted into the machine room. The entire room was a warren of pipes and strange equipment, all hooked together and terminating in two separate nests, or pods, facing each other, which occupied the very center of the cavernous space. The room seemed to take up the entire top floor of the house, minus the anteroom where their clothes had been removed. Ting helped Rufus to one of the pods while Gabrielle helped Harold to the other.

"Ting and Gabrielle have been trained to prepare and attend young men undergoing treatment so you must allow them to do their job. I'm sure some of what they do will seem strange to you. Just know it is all quite necessary for the harmonious and effective release of the excess energy blocking your chi." The maids slipped rubber bits into each man's mouth and tightened the straps behind their heads. "The mouth pieces are for your safety and comfort."

At this point, both men were relaxed enough from the sedatives in the tea so as to be unconcerned by the preparations. Mei knew once the "treatment" was underway, they would not want to stop, even after the sedative properties of the tea had worn off. When they came back for later appointments, and come back they would, they would need less and less of the drug before entering the machine room. It was only necessary to break down societal conditioning on the first few visits.

The maids were attaching the belts and cuffs, which would help to keep them moored in place and restrained. In this way, there would be no accidental removal of the equipment necessary to extract their energy and convert it into electricity.

Early on in her experiments, Mei had been concerned that she was actually extracting chi from her young subjects. The thought produced many sleepless nights, as the extraction of a person's chi would be very wrong, indeed. She soon came to realize, however, that up to a certain age, a young man's sexual energy was renewable. In fact, the more he spent, the more he acquired in its place.

Therefore, one could argue, she'd written, *the mechanical extraction of energy from the postadolescent male body is beneficial to his overall sexual health and well-being. Further experimentation is needed to determine the age at which the process becomes a hamper, rather than a benefit, to the subjects' powers of sexual rejuvenation.*

Plus, of course, it had the added benefit of powering her home. No more gaslights for her. She was even working on a time-saving invention for laundering linens and clothing, not to mention her new idea of a kind of electric music box. After all, there would always be an unending supply of sexually charged young men; they were a renewable resource.

Harold and Rufus had been settled into their respective pods and smoked goggles had been placed over their eyes. Their attendants were just fastening them into the optimal position. Their wrists were restrained at their waist belts so they would not be able to touch themselves or disconnect any of the rods, wires or tubing soon to be attached. Rufus seemed to be complaining again.

"Honestly, Rufus, dear, the way you carry on one would believe you had not a care in the world for your own life force." Mei soothed his brow. "Shall I personally take charge of your preparation? Would that ease your mind?" She could feel the tension in his arms lessen. "That will be all, Ting. You may see to the machine's readiness. There, there now, Rufus," she cooed as she positioned his legs, knees spread and supported above the level of his heart. She stroked his inner thighs as she fastened them with the soft silk cords.

His building erection did not go unnoticed. The more securely she fastened him to the pod, the harder and longer his cock became. Rubber chest bands were secured and finally his waist belt was tied down to eyelets in the pod, as well. Mei glanced toward Harold's pod to find that Gabrielle had reached the same point in his preparations,

"Now, this part may be a tad uncomfortable," she said to Rufus, "but just know that it is all in your best interest and any slight discomfort you experience now will be converted soon enough to pleasure."

Coating a shiny metal rod with lanolin, she slowly inserted it in the young man's anus, producing a series of squeals and grunts from behind his gag. She had fastened him well to the pod so there was very little movement of his buttocks, as he tried in vain to escape the penetration. Of course, once the rod had been seated inside him, he calmed. They always calmed once the insertion was complete.

A mass of rubber tubing, wires and straps hung above the pod, awaiting placement. Using more lanolin, she inserted his stiff cock into a rubber sleeve. She pulled it down to his testicles, allowing the head of his penis to remain just above the upper edge of the sleeve, which she corseted tightly with black silk cord.

Flexible rubber tubing hung from a small steam-driven bellows directly above the pod. These she affixed, with spirit gum, to the young man's nipples, holding the tubing in place until the glue had dried and created a fast bond to his skin. Similar tubing was pulled down from above. This larger diameter tubing was affixed, in the same manner, over the twin globes of Rufus's balls.

Mei noted the amount of clear, viscous, fluid leaking from the eye of his cock and, returning to the young man's buttocks, she removed a plunger from the end of the rod, transforming it into a hollow metal tube allowing access to his interior. More fluid leaked from the young man's cock as she prepared the insert, which was one side of the twin hearts of the collection process. Attaching a small pompom of fluffy cotton fibers to the end of a zinc rod, she dipped it in a brine solution and inserted the whole affair into the now hollow tube inside the young man's bottom. She knew it had been seated correctly when Rufus grunted loudly and his trussed cock jumped and quivered. A heavy copper wire attached to the end of the steel rod wound it's way up into the bowels of the machine and disappeared quickly from view.

"Almost done now, Mr. Hamilton. One final preparation left and then your treatment will begin" she cooed to him and placed a chaste kiss on his forehead, calming him, although she could hear him whimpering behind his gag. To the head of his cock, she fitted a cotton cap, soaked in brine. Two small copper wires extended from the fabric and were also lost to sight in the massive machine. This completed the preparations required to harvest the electricity his body would expend during the "treatment."

Checking on Gabrielle's progress, she noted that Harold's penis cap was just being fitted to him. Once his preparation was complete, she laid a kiss upon his brow, as well, and stepped to a panel of levers, switches and buttons. Throwing the first pair of switches started the bellows, which produced a strong suction through the rubber tubing attached to the subjects' nipples and balls. Pressing a pair of small green buttons started a pulsing sensation within the suction. Harold began to giggle behind his bit and Rufus grunted once, tensed and relaxed.

Opening a pressure gauge, the rubber sheathes encasing the two men's cocks filled with air, squeezing the captive flesh. Once each corseted bladder was sufficiently filled, she set the pressure to hold steady. She threw twin levers, starting the pumping action of each sheath. "Soon your minds will be rid of those unwanted impure thoughts which plague you," she said. Of course it wasn't true. The treatment would instill a level heretofore unknown in their preoccupation with thoughts of a sexual nature, prompting them to seek "treatment" again and again.

Soon, their bodies began to twitch and their grunts grew louder. An arc of blue electricity could be seen at the other end of the room. Cautioning the attendants to assure the pompoms inside the boys' bottoms and the caps on their cockheads were kept continually moistened with the brine solution, Mei made her way through the warren of pipes making up the machine until she reached the site of the electrical spark.

Alessandro Volta was a genius! His experiments in batteries and electrical energy, along with her studies of Galvani's work, had given her the idea to harvest and store electrical energy. She watched as a blue spark of electricity danced from the large copper plate, at the terminus of the machine, through a huge brine-filled glass tank, to the zinc plate on its bottom. The tank acted as the receptacle of the electricity and became the electric cell, which powered her house.

One healthy young man hooked up to a pod for a period of two hours could easily provide enough energy to power the lighting in her home for a day or two. If both pods were filled, the amount of energy could double, or better. Of course, the amount of electricity harvested depended on each boy's stamina and level of sexual voracity. Some subjects produced almost twice the amount of electrical energy as others.

Noting the extraction was running smoothly she once again retired to her writing. She would return toward the end of their cycle.

Back at her desk, she marveled at the strength of the light now shining on her writing.

* * *

The almost limitless amount of power produced by the average young man's libido is amazing. If the force were put to a good cause, rather than simply the random thoughts and actions of the young male, as he matures, one marvels at what might be developed. It is unimaginable that I should be the first to discover and develop this potential. However, due to the sensitive nature of my experimentation, it would be difficult to publish my findings. I'm sure others are experiencing the same problems disseminating their work, as well. Oh, if only we few scientists knew of each other and might collaborate...

The lamp on her desk grew brighter still, until the glass bulb containing it exploded, surprising Mei such that her chair toppled over backward, propelling her to the floor and keeping her from sustaining more than two small cuts from the shattering glass.

Racing back to the third floor, she found that the machine initially seemed to be functioning at optimum levels. However, taking a closer look at Rufus, she saw the way his gluteal muscles rhythmically convulsed around the metal tube protruding from his bottom. His hips strained against the restraints holding him to the pod and a thick sheen of perspiration coated his body. His hands flexed and formed fists, over and over and, with nostrils flaring, he panted behind his gag.

Harold appeared to be undergoing what she had come to realize was a normal experience in his pod. Obviously in the throes of sexual fervor, his body was laboring in its continuous climb toward the fulfillment of ultimate pleasure. But Rufus appeared to be in a sexual frenzy. So intense were his physical labors that Mei feared for his personal safety—surely for the safety of the machine, as she now realized that it was just this level of intensity that caused the power to spike so danger-ously.

The insidious nature of the machine was such that it sent its subjects on an ineffable journey toward ultimate sexual fulfill-ment, but didn't allow consummation of that goal—not until power down, which was controlled by the attendant.

A decision had to be made and made quickly. Mei rushed to the glass tank and checked the gauge. It showed a full cell with the needle well on its descent into the red. Quickly, she raced back to the pod controls and simultaneously pressed two buttons. One button forced Harold into his much-needed climax. The other button was the emergency shutdown for the other pod. It stopped all stimulation in Rufus's pod completely.

Harold moaned into his gag and, with a twitch of his cock, the force of his semen propelled the bit of fabric covering his penis away and, in four spurts, coated the outside of the deflating rubber sleeve encasing his penis.

Rufus, on the other hand, could be clearly heard to scream, "No!" behind his gag. There was no decrease in the tension in his body. He fought to keep himself on the edge of orgasm, striving for that very necessary release of sexual tension.

"I'm sorry," Mei said as she ripped the cotton cap off his very purple cockhead. Using a small pair of embroidery scis-sors, she cut the cord of the rubber cock corset and peeled it away from his very hard shaft. "The machine was overloading. I had to shut it off." He moaned behind his gag.

On her knees, by his pod, she quickly enclosed the top half of his shaft in her mouth; he was too large for her to take him fully. Wrapping her tongue around the head of his cock, she sucked and swirled until she could feel his cock expand even more inside her mouth. With a no-nonsense motion she twisted the rod in his rear end, nudging the small gland inside him with purpose.

The force of his climax was something for which she was unprepared. The first release of ejaculate pounded against the back of her throat, almost making her gag. She quickly removed her mouth and watched him spurt his seed into the air.

Mei looked at Rufus and saw visions of full cells, stacked up and awaiting use. She removed his goggles and unfastened his bit gag. As his body calmed, she said, "My dear young man, in my professional opinion, you would do well to seek treatment twice a week, at the very least. You have built up quite an excess of energy, which, for your own safety, should be tapped at once!"

He blinked up at her from his pod and smiled.

LUCIFER EINSTEIN AND THE CURIOUS CASE OF THE CARNAL CONTRAPTION

Tracey Shellito

I set the ornithopter down on the patio with hardly a bump. Earnshaw's broad smile and pat on my shoulder signaled her pleasure in my almost perfect landing. The umbrella-like lift mechanism gave a final double thump as I cut the power and steam hissed as I released the pressure. Only then did the under butler hurry forward with the disembarkation ladder. Once the device was set, he scurried to close the doors on our workroom lest the demon dust get into the delicate mechanisms stored there. Morrison, my butler and de facto housekeeper in my absence, opened the ornithopter door and offered a hand to assist first Earnshaw then myself to alight, then walked a respectful pace behind us back into the laboratoire.

"Has Monsieur Dupin returned yet?"

"No, madam, he sent word that he has been detained by the Prefect of Police. It seems there might be a mystery that could use his particular talents."

"Excellent! Then we shall likely have work soon. Prepare the thinking room." Earnshaw rubbed her gloved hands in anticipation and we shared a complicit smile. "I hope this case will be as fascinating at the last, old friend. Forging that letter to replace the purloined original was the most fun I've had in ages." I peeled off my own gloves and shed flying goggles and jacket, accepting a basin and towel from Collins, the under butler, to wash the grime from my face. Earnshaw scooped up my discards and bustled away to her own rooms, via the laundry.

"Madam has a visitor."

I fixed Morrison with my most piercing glare. I wasn't expecting anyone. Anybody I considered a friend was well aware that this was my personal time, when I went riding or practiced flying. Morrison's face showed thinly veiled annoyance that could mean only one thing. Mother. Bugger!

"Where have you put her?"

"In the solar, madam. I gave her to assume you would be somewhat later returning than is your usual wont. Situating her thus meant she would be unlikely to hear the ornithopter's arrival. You might perhaps have several moments to change your attire..."

"Tedious man, why on earth should my daughter need to change... Mother of Mercy, what are you wearing?" Morrison rolled his eyes and hurried away from the approaching harridan. "What mannish monstrosity is that?"

"My flying garb, Mother. What are you doing here? I thought you were assisting in some wedding preparations?"

"That is perfectly true. And it is also my reason for being here. Much as it galls me to admit it, I need your help."

It isn't often I get to see her squirm, so I folded my arms across my ample bosom and tapped an elegantly booted foot and waited.

"Hell-born child, your father named you well!"

"Mother!"

She harrumphed a few times then spat it out. "Cressida has refused to marry Sir Douglas."

"What? She was positively rabid for it a month ago. I remember everyone thought she was pregnant...."

"Yes, well, it would appear not. But things have taken an uncomfortable turn. It would seem that three nights ago the girl received, shall we say, a visitation?"

"Mother, what are you talking about?"

"Luci, please don't make me speak of it! You have to come back with me now, today. You have to hear her with your own ears. I am at a complete loss. Perhaps you can find some way, with your ratiocination, to solve the mystery."

How could I refuse? As I sat beside Earnshaw, opposite my mother, on the passenger deck of the dirigible, I considered the known facts.

Cressida Waltham had been a contemporary of mine in finishing school. Dreadfully spoiled, she was a daddy's little darling who could have whatever she wanted. And what she wanted had been Morton de Witt, my cradle betrothed. The girl had been positively addicted to the pleasures of the bedchamber, an awful scandal at school. I hadn't believed he'd fall for her dubious charms, yet faithlessly he had. Needless to say, mother had called our arrangement off and I'd been married to my dear Ferdie. But my happiness was short-lived. Ferdie had been run over by one of the newfangled automobiles on the way to the railway station to join me for our honeymoon. After that, I had thrown myself into my researches and together with my childhood companion, the mute but ever faithful Earnshaw, had begun assisting the consulting detective Monsieur Dupin in Paris, as far away from the memories of both my lost loves as my allowance would let me flee.

That had been six months ago. I hadn't seen the witch Cressida from that day to this. Earnshaw had flown back and forth across the channel to fetch anything we needed from home, along with letters from Mother. Which was how I'd learned Cressida had got herself betrothed to the richest man in England. (Hardly a surprise. The only thing the gold-digging wench loved more than bed-sport was money.) I also learned that my mother had been asked to assist in the wedding preparations.

While Mother is an acknowledged social butterfly with all the right connections, I had been astonished to hear she'd lowered herself to helping the bitch who'd ruined my original nuptials. Clearly my absence had been more of a trial to her than I'd imagined. Or perhaps she had planned to upstage the little strumpet by showing that the Einsteins were a family who could rise above such defeats as we had suffered and be so much better than her? Whatever the reason, I was in no small part pleased to hear Cressida's own wedding was in some doubt. If I had to come back to this godforsaken country for something, at least it would be as a success—something she could not take away from me.

I watched the white cliffs of Dover drift by beneath us and cracked my knuckles thoughtfully while mother gave a moue of distaste. Earnshaw had already begun the diary of our adventure: *The Curious Case of the Carnal Contraption.* I was looking forward to it.

"I had been treated for hysteria before, but this machine was different," Cressida said, wringing her hands. I had partaken of several vibration devices from more than one quack purporting to be able to heal the grief of my bereavement; I knew whereof she spoke.

"Different? How so?" She cast a look in the direction of both our mothers staring avidly from across the room. I stood. "Perhaps you should show me where the incident took place? There might be clues."

She grasped the sop thankfully. "Yes, yes. I have not, that is I could not bear to... The room has been locked up since it happened."

"Excellent. Come, Earnshaw. There is not a moment to lose." Then when our mothers began to follow I raised a hand. "I'm afraid I must insist you remain. Too many feet trampling the scene could ruin vital evidence." Both looked crestfallen, but returned to their seats. Earnshaw and I followed Cressida to her bedroom, where she became markedly reluctant to unlock the door.

"The carnal engine is still within, isn't it?" She began to splutter protests. "Enough! There could be no other reason you would lock the door and forbid so much as a maid admittance. And the only reason you would think to refuse marriage to Sir Douglas is because you had something which would satisfy you more than he could."

Cressida's blush was eloquent. Earnshaw took the keys from her hand and unlocked the boudoir. When she attempted to be the first inside I held her back.

"No, this is for us to do. I did not speak lightly when I said that evidence could be eradicated. Simply tell me where you have secreted the device and Earnshaw and I will do the rest."

"You will not... Promise me you will not dismantle it!" Her lower lip was trembling. She truly was addicted to this infernal engine.

"Unless it is necessary to establish its provenance, I will not." She looked relieved. "But you must immediately tell Sir Douglas that you were merely having cold feet and that the wedding is still on. There is no reason why you cannot enjoy the pleasures he provides as well as this contraption if you are circumspect. If men were to discover how well a mechanical device could pleasure a woman, do you not think all such instruments would be destroyed? How then would the ladies suffering from hysteria find surcease from their problems?" I could see my final words were falling on deaf ears. Once told that she could have both and whatever his money could provide her, Cressida had no need of the bigger picture. She never was the brightest student.

"It is in my wardrobe. A hatbox with pink stripes."

"We shall find it. Go now. We both have work to do."

Earnshaw locked the door behind us once we were inside. The room was dim, the curtains half drawn leaving a dusky light that emphasized the musky aroma of sex. I could not begin to imagine how many times she had used the device on herself to leave the room smelling so ripe. While I ignited a gas lamp, the better to see what evidence might be gleaned, Earnshaw sought out the hatbox.

I needed no magnifying glass to see the muddy footprints on the floor leading from the drapes to the foot of the bed. But I was surprised by their size; they were hardly the marks of an average man's boot soles. The lock of the window had clearly been jimmied, and quite expertly from outside, a small hole—probably cut with a diamond-tipped scribe—revealing where a hand had been inserted while the intruder had squatted on the generous ledge to do the deed. As I examined the pane, something blew across my vision. I espied a rope, dangling from some mooring on the roof above, down which the intrepid visitant had climbed and presumably the way by which he had returned. That implied that the miscreant was one of the household staff or a guest here for the wedding.

I turned from my thoughts to find that Earnshaw had been

successful in unearthing the carnal contraption and had set
it out upon the rumpled bed. I forgot all my suppositions as I
drifted close to examine the find.

"Oh my..."

A selection of softly padded leather straps would affix the
device securely to the...victim hardly seemed the correct word.
Clearly the engine was a device solely aimed at a woman's pleasure. A carefully carved phallus of wood sheathed in the softest
leather could be cranked by means of a handle to penetrate
the one to be pleasured at a speed that suited the participant
or employer. There was even a key movement, that Earnshaw
ably demonstrated, which would allow hands free use until
the clockwork mechanism ran down and would plunder the
cunny of the pleasure-seeker with all the regularity of a piston.
I found myself blushing hot just to think of it. And neither had
the external application been neglected. A small brush of barely
stiffened bristles was positioned correctly to stroke the willing
participant and encourage the pearl from its shell. I felt wetness
start between my legs and rushed to the privy to take care of
myself. But all the time I rubbed away my need I was imagining
the wonderful and dreadful engine about its work upon me....

By the time I returned my bloomers were soaked. Earnshaw
had thoughtfully laid out a pair of Cressida's clean drawers and
I gratefully divested myself of my sodden underclothes and hid
them amongst the detritus of the bedroom, knowing full well
that the maids would dispose of all when I allowed them access
to the crime scene, thus leaving my pilfering and my indiscre-
tion undiscovered.

Earnshaw had replaced the disconcerting device in the
hatbox when I was once more able to continue, but she had not
closed the lid. She beckoned me over and pointed out a series of
markings that I had to squint to make out in the dim light. Until

that moment, I confess, I had been thinking of confiscating the device in the name of science and research. But what I saw made me think again.

"Mark VI! Good gracious, do you suppose there are more of them out there?" Earnshaw nodded, her expression serious. "And since the intruder is a member of this household..."

There would be other victims!

And so we began our investigation in earnest. I questioned every female member of the household and every guest. Such proved necessary as our second find was dubbed the Mark V....

"I was in the pantry and the 'gentleman,' though I don't know as I should rightly use the word, came up behind me. I wears them bloomers without a crotch, that just lace onto the garter belt, though I don't know how he knew! He bent me over the chopping block, flipped up my skirts and gave me a right seeing to with his device. Strapped on himself, it were. Plundered both my holes! I was all fit to scream the house down, only it felt so good. And what with my old man having the trouble with his old fella, well, it's been some time since I last had the pleasure of being ridden.... He left it behind when he'd finished. The wedgie was hollow like. My husband has been using it to pleasure me ever since. 'Ere, you won't be taking it with you, will you?"

"My husband was in the smoking room taking cigars and brandy with his lodge mates. He's grand poo-bah, you know! I had retired to bed, knowing it would be a good many hours before he joined me and had slipped a few drops of laudanum in my nightcap."

"Nessa!"

"Yes, sorry. Easily distracted, I know. I woke up to find my wrists and ankles fastened to the bedposts and my nightgown raised to my neck. Luckily the night was warm or I could have taken a chill! Anyway, I found a gag in my mouth, so screaming was out of the question. I couldn't see the fellow clearly; the lights were out, the curtains partly drawn and only a crescent moon outside. He seemed slight and had small, clever hands. He stood at the foot of the bed for quite some time just looking at my nude body in the moonlight, then he produced an ostrich feather from a bag and proceeded to stroke me with it. It was... I liked it a great deal."

"Nothing mechanical?"

"I was getting to that! Next he produced an ermine mitten and began to rub my breasts very, very gently, paying extra attention to the nipples and the sensitive undersides, while his tongue flickered into my armpits and navel. I was transported with bliss."

And I was wet again. If this continued I was going to have to start carrying around a bag of clean undergarments. "What happened next?"

"When he fitted little suction manipulators to my breasts I thought I should die of delight. By the time he brought out his device I was sopping wet and he didn't have to work hard to enter me. The contraption clamped to the bedposts and extended to reach, then after he'd inserted it, he wound the key tight and flicked a switch and I was pounded to ecstasy. It was just as well he'd put the gag on, I'd have screamed for England. When I came to myself he'd untied my hands and left the devices. I've used them all many times when I know my husband will be late home. Unfortunately I overwound the spring recently and the main device is ruined, but the suction devices still work and I'm being extracareful with them. I can come now from just them alone, if I'm thinking about the other device. Would you like to see them?"

Lady Vanessa pulled out a rifle case and withdrew the items in question. MARK II, this read. "Binkie would never think to look in here. Hates hunting, thinks it's a beastly sport. Oh, Earnshaw, you darling! I think you've fixed it...."

We found the fourth device in a most unexpected place. Earnshaw's cousin was the under butler to the Waltham household and she made much of her relative in her written missives, taking frequent side trips when she came to England on her errands for me. I had been apprised of the fact that he had a liking for gentlemen. Since he seemed a likeable sort, it was in no wise my place to judge his proclivities, no matter what polite society thought. Especially since I had spent the last five hours fantasying so hotly about intimate acts with clockwork and mechanical devices!

Wilkins lived in a garret above the coach house, with the coachman, who was of a like persuasion. The tender way they had with each other reminded me of Earnshaw's careful handling of my person. I put such thoughts from my mind as her cousin's tale unfolded.

"I would not normally discuss such things with a gently bred lady, but my cousin says you are of broad mind and will not judge me, so, in light of your investigation I shall tell you exactly what transpired."

I settled myself carefully on the hassock, mindful of the effects others' tales had had upon my anatomy.

"Jim and I have been together nearly a year and hope to be so for life. Our only sadness is that he could never experience the full joy of total union as he is, if he'll pardon my saying so, a much smaller man in some departments than would be considered average. While he can gain pleasure from using his mouth on me, or me on him, he could not rod me as I did him, as he did not have the length. All that changed a week ago. We had just returned from our daily labors when he found a package addressed to him on the table in the modest kitchen of our apartments. When he opened it... Well, I'll let him tell the tale."

Jim produced said package. Still surrounded with the tattered remains of the brown waxed paper and string that had sealed it against casual gaze, the lid lifted to reveal a harness of straps not unlike a horse's bridle. Yet clearly it was made to strap upon a hipless man. And fixed where the bit might be was a glorious phallus made of rubber, nearly ten inches in length, lovingly molded in all the particulars and bending in exactly the right way for rear entry. We all of us observed it with some awe, as one might Michelangelo's *David*. It was a thing of beauty and artistry. And what is more, there was a mechanical contraption attached to it.

"This pump inflates the inner bladder to hold me firm inside so I can feel everything through the hollow walls as if I were doing the penetrating," Jim told me as proudly as if he'd invented the device himself. "And that mechanism gently pulls and twists me as I plunge in and out, so that I gain as much satisfaction as from the best hand job. The device is a marvel!"

"They left these too." Wilkins displayed a pair of gloves whose palms were studded with rubber blobs and nodules. He stroked his fingers over them suggestively. No need to explain their use. While his partner fucked him he could stroke himself with these sensuously surfaced gloves and bring his own ejaculation. The pair were growing hard and excited just talking about their gift. Hurriedly, Earnshaw and I left (having noted the device was scribed MARK I), allowing the loving pair to make use of their windfall in private.

* * *

By the time evening fell the wedding was back on and Cressida's thankful family offered us a bed for the night. By dinner's end we had interviewed all the female staff and every female guest. We had uncovered nine different devices: I–X though we were missing Mark VIII. We had only found one given to gentlemen. And were no closer to discovering the mysterious benefactor or his or her motivations. I had my suspicions, but did not share them. I had the feeling the whereabouts of the missing device and the identity of its owner were about to be revealed and prematurely spilling the truth might spoil what lay in store.

I helped Earnshaw comb and braid her hair for bed then surprised her when she gathered mine up for the same treatment. "I think I shall leave it unbound tonight." I put on my satin sleep mask, then she helped me into bed and arranged my hair over my pillow, turned down the gaslights and slipped away to her room. When I was alone, I wriggled out of my nightdress, careful not to disarrange my hair, and pushed it under the bed. Then I waited.

The house was long quiet and I in a languorous doze, when I finally heard the scratch of a diamond stylus on the windowpane and a few moments later the window was unlatched and pushed up against the sash. I lay perfectly still, hardly daring to breath. Only when the intruder was completely inside the room, the window closed against hue and cry, and I sensed the person at the foot of my bed did I speak.

"I have been expecting you. What will it be? The Mark VIII?"

For a moment, my sex crusader froze. This was the culmination of all the experiments. To be found out now spelled disaster. I decided for my uncertain swain.

"I am a woman who has been without intimate company for

over six months. I will not turn you away nor expose you. Rather I am eager for what you offer. I submit voluntarily. Uncover me and see if I do not speak the truth."

The intruder ripped back the bedclothes to reveal my nude body. I heard breath catch, then bags were opened and equipment prepared while I awaited my fate. Silk scarves tied my hands gently to the bedposts. A hand with quick clever fingers stroked the hair from my brow and laid a kiss upon my lips, before beginning to stroke down my body, grazing hard nipples, taunt stomach, quivering thighs. Their touch was more welcome than mink, more delicate than feathers, more knowing than any machine. They knew exactly where to touch, how much and for how long. When my moans of pleasure threatened to wake others, those lips found mine again and silenced me, first with firm pressure, then with the invasion of a fennel scented serpent that jousted with my own for possession of my mouth.

While one hand switched to kneading my breasts, a phallus more carefully molded than that given to Wilkins, more powerfully vibrated than Cressida's, driven by a precision clockwork mechanism, thrust inside my hot wetness, after those same clever fingers parted my lower lips. My lover rose above me, raising my legs and hooking them over strong shoulders, as the mechanism shook and shuddered and stroked the entire length of the shaft inside me.

Not content with a single penetration, I felt myself opened further and was plundered at the same time from behind, all the measurements precise to me; a questing wet finger tempting my puckered rosebud and rimming it round and round while gently pressing within.

At last, when I thought I should explode from pleasure, when I thought there could be nothing to surpass this, an implement covered with nodules of varying size and stiffness rasped my aching clit. I shrieked out my fulfillment with the name of my nemesis, gushing and drenching my lover as I came.

When they threw open the door, I was properly covered with bedclothes and quite alone. I apologized shamefacedly for waking them.

"A dream."

"Too much rich food and a strange bed most like," my mother mused with a sniff, taking herself back to bed.

"More than that surely," Cressida's mother disagreed. "It sounded more as if you were being murdered."

"Or having the best sex of your life," Cressida said ushering her mother out with a smile for me over her shoulder.

When they were gone, the intruder slid out from beneath my bed, clutching my nightdress.

"So that's where it got to. Be a darling and lock the door so we won't be interrupted next time. What, you didn't think there'd be a next time? Six months is a long dry season and I have an itch you've only begun to scratch. Now lock the door then come back to bed. And you'd better have a gag in that bag of tricks, or this is going to be a very frustrating night."

When I announced I was leaving that morning and had solved the mystery, the women were baffled.

"Who is the miscreant?" Lady Vanessa asked.

"That I cannot tell you. Revealing the culprit would mean exposing all of you. I have been sworn to keep their identity secret, on the understanding that they will never visit themselves upon unsuspecting or unwilling victims again. I think that is the best result we can hope for, given the scandal otherwise."

At that there were a good many uncomfortable nodding heads.

"And you can look forward to a steady supply of like devices appearing for sale quite soon. I think I have convinced the experimenter there is a market for these carnal engines. All enquiries can be made through me at my laboratoire in Paris. An appropriate city for the commercial production of such devices, I'm sure you'll agree."

"But what about punishment? Should they be allowed to go free? They almost ruined my daughter's marriage!" Cressida's mother exclaimed.

"Never fear. I have seen to it that they will be punished and the punishment will fit the crime. Now you must forgive me, I have an airship to catch."

Earnshaw slammed the luggage into the boot of our rented automobile, assisted me to a seat, then climbed behind the wheel. I set a hand possessively on her thigh as we drove away in a roar and whoosh of steam.

"You *will* be crafting a Mark VIII device to your particular specifications the moment we get home, won't you, darling?"

She spared me a look, but didn't take her small clever hands off the wheel for a moment as she nodded. The merest hint of a blush crept up her cheeks toward her goggles.

THE SUCCUBUS

Elizabeth Schechter

In the parlor, there is a portrait of Madame, painted when she was a shy young miss of seventeen. She is looking over her shoulder, and her midnight hair tumbles down her back in a profusion of curls. The uninitiated might think that this house, which has come to be called the House of the Sable Locks, was named for that portrait and for Madame's glorious spill of hair. But that is not so; Madame's hair is more silver than sable now, and there is another reason for the name. The uninitiated never go farther than the parlor, never know that there is another world beyond the doors that lead into the rear of the house. They think that Madame is simply a woman of independent means, the widow of a rich, albeit eccentric, inventor. They do not know the truth. They do not know about us.

The House of the Sable Locks is famous, but only in a rarefied circle. Certain men meet at their clubs and whisper to each other about the delights that they find behind our doors. There is the second floor, where those who prefer women can gather. Or the third floor, wherein those who prefer men can find what they seek. And then there is the fourth floor, where I can be found. But I get ahead of my story.

The "Sable Locks" refer not to a woman's crowning glory, but to the exquisitely wrought and enameled locks that adorn the collars of the men who frequent our halls. They come here at first uncertain of what they will find, knowing only the whispers of their peers. They meet with Madame in private, and no one speaks of what happens behind those closed doors. But when that meeting is over the gentlemen either leave the house, never to return, or Madame takes them on a tour. It will be the first and last time they walk the halls as free men; when next they arrive at the house, they will be escorted to the servants' quarters. There, they will be stripped of clothing and jewelry, hooded, gagged and collared. Thus rendered silent and anonymous and wearing only their locked collars, the bearers of the Sable Lock make their way to their chosen rooms and to the pleasures and torments that await them there. They never know who the other men are, or of what station they might be. The man that they pass in the hallway might be a member of the House of Lords, or the son of the butcher, or even their own brother. No one knows for certain except for Madame.

And me.

The fourth floor is usually quiet, with only the hum of machinery and the distant voices from the floors below. The men do not return to the fourth floor after their initial encounter with me. They desire something more familiar, more in keeping with their personal fantasies. More safe. So I wait, alone, and the silent servants tend to my needs. This evening will be different. I know it already. I can hear Madame's familiar step on the stair, and another, heavier step with her.

She enters first, the train of her evening gown sweeping the floor as she moves to the table and lights the lamp. The man lingers in the door, peering into the gloom. He wears pristine evening dress, and the lamplight picks out the gold links in his watch-chain and the gleam of the ruby on his left hand. The walls have already whispered his secrets to me: the second son of a duke, one who was never expected to take the reins of power. One who came, all unexpected, into an inheritance that was never meant to be his. His older brother was dead of typhoid, gone without a son to succeed him, and so the younger son was now Earl Hathaway. It was no surprise to us that the late, lamented Reginald Warwick, Earl Hathaway had died without issue—he had also borne the collar and lock in this house and had shown a definite preference for the third floor. It will be interesting to see what the new Lord Hathaway prefers. His name, the walls have told me, is Nigel.

"You can come in," Madame says. "She won't bite you." She laughs and leaves the lamp to go to the far wall and the switches there. She throws them, one at a time, and light floods the room.

I hear him gasp, and I know what he sees. The ceilings in this room are high, and although they try to hide it with draperies, you can still see the machines that tower overhead, disappearing into the shadows above the lights. The machines hum and churn, gears half the size of a man moving in the eternal dance that gives me life. Occasionally they release puffs of fragrant steam into the air, making the entire room warmer than would normally be considered comfortable. There is very little furniture in the room, most of it covered with drapery against dust and future need. And then there is me. Shining silver and chrome, gleaming brass and copper, I lie in wait, reclined on the wide couch as might a goddess whilst she awaited her worshippers.

"But...it's clockwork!" he blurts out, stepping into the room. He looks around, expecting to see a living woman. But, of course, there is no one else in the room.

Madame sniffs slightly. "Of course she is. I did explain that to you, did I not?"

Lord Hathaway has the grace to look embarrassed, "You did, but...the others all look...alive. This one..." He gestures wildly.

"She was the first, created by my late husband," Madame says, walking over to my couch. She brushes her nails over my shoulder and continues, "The others came later, and I refined the forms to make them more...approachable. Despite her form, the Succubus is the most complex of all the automatons."

"How can that be? It looks like a statue!" He takes a step toward the couch and points at me. "It is a statue!"

Madame runs her fingers over my gleaming silver skull, "Oh, this is just the focal point, Your Lordship. The Succubus encompasses this room."

He looks around, his eyes wide. "The whole room?"

"The whole of this floor, actually. As I said, she is very complex." Madame makes her way back to the wall and stands near the bell-rope. "Now, it is customary for the first appointment to be with the Succubus. Did your brother not tell you this?"

Lord Hathaway shakes his head. "All Reg told me was that I would not believe what I found here. He wouldn't say more." He swallows, looking nervously at the figure on the couch and then back at Madame, "Is it safe?"

Madame laughs. "My dear sir, you'll be as safe here as in your own mother's arms, if that is your desire."

He looks at her sharply. "What does that mean?"

Madame just smiles. "You've seen what we offer. Surely it's

no surprise to you that there are some who prefer an element of
risk. Don't you agree?"

He does, although I doubt that any would see it but me.
His breathing quickens, ever so slightly. The flush in his cheeks
heightens, just a touch. He looks at me again, studying me,
silent. After a long moment, he turns back to Madame. "What
do I have to do?"

She draws from the reticule that hangs from her wrist one
of the shining silver collars, the black lock dangling from the
end. She smiles at my soon-to-be paramour, "Take off your
clothes."

He balks, of course. They always do. Disrobe in front of a
woman? Unthinkable! Even though the woman is the propri-
etress of the most exclusive brothel in London, they simply
can't. I think that Madame enjoys their discomfort, and that is
why she does it. Eventually, she tires of his protests and rings for
one of the silent servants.

"Lay your clothing there," Madame says and points to a
chair near the door. "The servant will guard the door and make
certain that you are undisturbed. And I will have a room made
up for you."

Nigel looks startled. "Will that be necessary?"

Madame smiles. "The Succubus likes to take her time." Then
she leaves, and the door closes behind her with a soft thump.
Nigel stares at the door for a moment, then starts to unbutton his
waistcoat, turning away from me in what must be an automatic
gesture. He has already removed his tie and unbuttoned his high
collar so that Madame could lock the collar around his throat.

A voice is nothing but air through valves. I can have any
voice I choose. This time, I choose a girl's voice, light and gentle.
"I can still see you," I say softly. "You needn't try to hide. I like
to watch."

He spins, startled, looking for the owner of the voice. "Who...who said that?"

I answer, "I am the Succubus. And my eyes are throughout this room. So you need not try to hide from me."

"You speak?" He starts edging toward the door.

"I do a great many things. Isn't that why you're here?" I pause, and he stops moving. Good. Time to begin. "Do you enjoy being frightened, Nigel?"

"No!" he says quickly. "How do you know my name?"

"I know many things about you, Nigel," I keep my voice soft and low. "I know you seek an escape from the madness that your life has become since your brother died and you assumed his title. I know that you wish for a return to the carefree days of being the younger son. Your life has become structured, regimented. You want excitement."

In actuality, I know none of these things. I do know that he is the younger son, much younger than his brother. Younger sons are allowed some leeway in their dealings, and it is all overlooked since they will not bear the title. And...he is here. If he were looking for a mistress, he would be at the opera or the theater. If he desired a simple coupling, a push-in-the-dark-here's-a-farthing-never-see-the-girl-again, he would be in Whitechapel. He wants neither of these. He wants some excitement, but something that carries no risk of scandal. I can tell now that he needs something more than a simple tryst.

The chair hits him right behind the knees, and he sits down hard, the breath exploding out of him. I have him in a trice, bindings snapping closed around his legs, waist and chest. Cables catch his wrists and pull them into position for the bindings that fix his arms to the chair. He is mine.

He struggles for a moment, opens his mouth to protest, and his breath catches when he sees the mechanical arm rising from the floor between his feet. The knife blade at the end shines in the harsh lights, the edge glittering as I move it this way and that. "It is very sharp, I assure you," I say. "Do not struggle."

"What are you doing?" he whispers, looking like a bird facing a snake, his glassy eyes never leaving the blade. I don't answer, lowering the knife back toward the floor. I wait a moment, letting his breathing quicken, then slip the blade into the leg of his trousers, brushing against his skin before I begin cutting. His fine trousers part easily as I work my way slowly up the seam, tracing lightly over the inside of his thighs as my blade travels up each leg. He moans, closing his eyes and trying oh-so-valiantly not to move or even to breathe as the blade lays his skin bare. His arms are ticklish, and he yelps as I cut away his fine silk shirt and trace the blue veins under his skin. When I am done, his skin is shining with sweat, his breathing quick and shallow. His cock, freed at last from its linen and wool prison, stands proudly like a soldier at attention.

I pitch my voice so that it seems to come from behind him, and add a puff of air so it seems to Nigel that I am whispering in his ear. "I see that you appreciate my handiwork."

My dear Nigel's only answer is a whimper; his eyelids flutter open, then he gasps in surprise to see the knife a scant inch from his nose. He swallows and struggles to control his need to pull away as I stroke his cheek with the knife, then move lower, tracing the pulsing vein in his throat. I prick his collarbone lightly, not even enough to raise a welt, then gently brush the blade over one of his erect nipples.

That is all it takes. Nigel wails like a girl, thrashing in his bonds while his seed splatters over his chest and legs and onto the floor. Then he goes limp, his eyes close, and his head lolls back as his chest heaves. I pull the knife arm back into the floor and consider my next move. I hadn't expected him to spend quite that quickly. As Madame said, I like to take my time. I don't think that I've even come close to exploring the full range of Nigel's possibilities.

I release his bonds and at the same time tip the chair forward, spilling him onto the ground like a child's rag doll. He lies there in the remains of his clothing and makes no protest when I lift him off the floor, holding him with a multitude of strong metal arms. I steady him and move him across the room; he does not notice until it is too late that I have a destination in mind. By the time he is aware of my purpose, I have already bent him over a table and drawn his arms back, wrapping his wrists in steel and binding them behind him. He struggles for a moment, but I hold him tightly in a lover's embrace and keep him in place. Nigel starts to shiver, whether from fear or the chill of the metal table I cannot tell. He closes his eyes tightly, and his cock twitches, starting to rise once again.

"Well," I murmur. "I certainly can't leave such a responsive toy unattended." A hose rises from the floor, and the end clamps around Nigel's semierect member and begins sucking; Nigel lets loose a high-pitched whine and thrusts his hips forward as much as my grip will allow.

It is times like this when I wish I had the ability to smile. "You enjoy fear," I say, my voice low. "How do you feel about pain?" I raise another of my arms, this one bearing a slender cane, and swish it experimentally over his head. His eyes shoot open, and he cranes his neck to see behind him, lifting his shoulders from the table.

"Now, now. None of that, my darling," I chide gently as a slender arm rises from within the surface of the table; it hooks into his collar and pulls him back down. He shivers more violently and squeezes his eyes closed again.

He screams at the first strike of the cane, pulling away from me so violently that I think for a moment that I have misjudged him. I hesitate and am pleasantly surprised when he shifts his hips, pushing his lovely bottom out as much as he can.

"More...more, please." His voice is harsh, and he moans as I trace the back of his knee with the tip of the cane.

"Of course, my darling. How could I refuse?"

He screams and moans as I lay a pattern of stripes over his buttocks and thighs, leaving livid red welts that promise to leave him unable to sit for any length of time, for days. I follow the cane with a velvet flogger, trailing the long, soft tails over his enflamed skin, then letting it fly to land with solid thumps against his ass, making him choke and gasp and beg for more. All the while, I tease him beneath the table, gently sucking and blowing on his cock, alternating pressure levels and suction, never letting him go long enough to reach his peak.

When at last he falls still, drenched in sweat, too exhausted to beg or struggle, I let the flogger tails trail over his limp fingers and whisper in his ear, "Shall I finish you, my darling?"

He moans and nods, twisting his wrists slightly and croaking out a single word: "Please?"

All he has to do is ask; I increase the suction and send another arm, this one wielding a rabbit-skin wand, to caress his bollocks and then slip between his legs and run up and down the marks on his thighs. His body tenses, like a harp-string wound far too tightly. When he finally releases, his climax is splendid: he pulls violently at his bonds, screaming his pleasure in his ruined voice. I drink his essence like the finest champagne, and call for the silent servants to come and collect my now-unconscious Lothario.

Three of them come, armed with blankets and baskets. I release Nigel to them, and two of them bundle him into a blanket and carry him away. The third collects the remains of

Nigel's clothing, the better to salvage his personal possessions. They will put Nigel to bed in the room Madame has ordered prepared, and in the morning, Nigel will breakfast with her and go on his way. In a week or two, I fully expect him to return. But I will not see him again. I know this; they never come back to see me. Nigel, I presume, would visit the Cruel Schoolmistress, or perhaps the Grand Inquisitor. They will provide him with the pleasures that he seeks, without the uncertainty of having to bow down to a machine that thinks and that enjoys toying with her paramours.

As for me, the silent servants will come in the middle of the night, clean the room and polish me until I shine. They will turn out the lights that illuminate the room, and they will leave me alone. The fourth floor will again be quiet, and I will wait, alone in the dark, until Madame again brings a gentleman to call.

ABOUT THE AUTHORS

JANINE ASHBLESS is the author of five books of paranormal and fantasy erotica published by Black Lace. Her short stories have been published in numerous Cleis anthologies including *Best Women's Erotica 2009*, *Sweet Love* and *Fairy Tale Lust*. She blogs about Minotaurs, Victorian art and writing dirty at janineashbless.blogspot.com.

Award-winning author KATHLEEN BRADEAN's stories can be found in *Spank!*, *The Best of Best Women's Erotica 2010*, EPIC Winner *Coming Together: Against the Odds* and Golden Crown Winner *Best Lesbian Fiction 2008*. She blogs weekly for Oh Get A Grip and reviews erotica monthly at EroticaRevealed.com and Erotica-Readers.com. More at KathleenBradean.blogspot.com.

DELILAH DEVLIN is an award-winning author with a rapidly expanding reputation for writing deliciously edgy stories with complex characters. More at DelilahDevlin.com

KANNAN FENG lives next door to Lake Michigan. She has previously been published by Circlet Press. Feng can be found at kannanfeng.wordpress.com.

JAY LAWRENCE is an expatriate Scot who currently makes her home near Vancouver, Canada. She is the author of various erotic novels and short stories that have appeared in publications on both sides of the Atlantic.

RENEE MICHAELS is interested in history, the paranormal, and the quirks that make us human. This is why she writes in several genres. She is widowed, with a daughter in college and a teenaged son who keeps her hopping.

TERESA NOELLE ROBERTS writes romance for the horny and erotica for the romantic, with a special love for paranormal tales. Her short fiction has appeared in numerous anthologies, including *Sweet Love: Erotic Fantasies for Couples* and *The Sweetest Kiss: Ravishing Vampire Erotica*. Her latest novel is *Foxes' Den*.

LISABET SARAI believes she was Victorian in a previous incarnation, given her lifelong attraction to turrets, corsets and lace-up boots. She has published six erotic novels including Victorian-themed *Incognito*, and dozens of shorter works. "Her Own Devices" is her first attempt at steampunk. Visit her online at lisabetsarai.com.

ELIZABETH SCHECHTER is a stay-at-home mom who lives in Central Florida, where she enjoys seeing the looks on the faces of the other playgroup moms when she answers the question "What do you do?" by describing herself as a pervy fetish writer. Elizabeth can be found online at elizabethschechter. blogspot.com.

TRACEY SHELLITO is the author of the crime novel *Personal Protection*. She has also appeared in anthologies for Torquere Press. She lives in Blackpool, Lancashire, UK. When not plotting fictional murders, she works in administration. She blogs on Amazon and Live Journal. Website: traceyshellito.moonfruit.com.

ELIAS A. ST. JAMES is a former high-school English teacher who has been writing for as long as he can remember. He lives with his partner of over fifteen years, their son and an aging cat.

ESSEMOH TEEPEE is a fiftysomething CEO in the UK. Writing erotica since 2005, he has a steadily growing following for his sensual stories and audio work. He is the creator of the unique Directed Erotic Visualization audio technique. Writing and downloadable audios can be found at his website smotp.com.

POE VON PAGE writes in Southern California where she lives with her family. Her most recent published erotica can be found at ForTheGirls.com. Contact her at PoeVonPage@gmail.com.

ABOUT
THE EDITOR

D. L. KING is a smut-writing and editing New Yorker who lives somewhere between the Wonder Wheel at Coney Island and the Chrysler Building. *Carnal Machines* is her third book with Cleis Press. She is the editor of *The Sweetest Kiss: Ravishing Vampire Erotica* and the Lambda Literary Award Finalist, *Where the Girls Are: Urban Lesbian Erotica*. She is also the editor of *Spank!* a Logical Lust anthology. D. L. King publishes and edits Erotica Revealed, the literary erotica book review site. The author of dozens of short stories, her work can be found in various editions of *The Mammoth Book of Best New Erotica, Best Women's Erotica, Best Lesbian Erotica*, as well as in titles such as *Fast Girls; Sex in the City: New York; Please, Ma'am; Sweet Love; Girl Crazy; Broadly Bound* and *Frenzy*, among others. She is the author of two novels of female domination and male submission, *The Melinoe Project* and *The Art of Melinoe*. Find out more at dlkingerotica.com.

Out of This World Romance

Steamlust
Steampunk Erotic Romance
Edited by Kristina Wright

Shiny brass and crushed velvet; mechanical inventions and romantic conventions; sexual fantasy and kinky fetish: this is a lush and fantastical world of women-centered stories and romantic scenarios, a first for steampunk fiction.
ISBN 978-1-57344-721-8 $14.95

The Sweetest Kiss
Ravishing Vampire Erotica
Edited by D.L. King

These sanguine tales give new meaning to the term "dead sexy" and feature beautiful bloodsuckers whose desires go far beyond blood.
ISBN 978-1-57344-371-5 $15.95

Dream Lover
Paranormal Tales of Erotic Romance
Edited by Kristina Wright

A potent potion of fun and sexy tales filled with male fairies and clairvoyant scientists, as well as darkly erotic tales of ghosts, shapeshifters and possession.
ISBN 978-1-57344-655-6 $14.95

Fairy Tale Lust
Erotic Fantasies for Women
Edited by Kristina Wright

Award-winning novelist and erotica writer Kristina Wright goes over the river and through the woods to find the sexiest fairy tales ever written.
ISBN 978-1-57344-397-5 $14.95

In Sleeping Beauty's Bed
Erotic Fairy Tales
By Mitzi Szereto

"Who can resist the erotic origins of fairy tales from Little Red to Rapunzel's long braid? Szereto knows her way around the mythic scholarship and the most outrageous sexual deviations in Pandora's Box." —Susie Bright
ISBN 978-1-57344-367-8 $16.95

Erotica for Every Kink

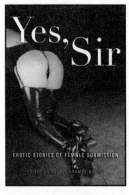

Yes, Sir
Erotic Stories of Female Submission
Edited by Rachel Kramer Bussel

The lucky women in *Yes, Sir* give up control to irresistibly powerful men who understand that dominance is about exulting in power that is freely yielded.
ISBN 978-1-57344-310-4 $15.95

Best Bondage Erotica
Edited by Alison Tyler

Always playful and dangerously explicit, these arresting fantasies grab you, tie you down, and never let you go.
ISBN 978-1-57344-173-5 $15.95

Best Bondage Erotica 2
Edited by Alison Tyler

From start to finish, these stories of women and men in the throes of pleasurable restraint will have you bound to your chair and begging for more!
ISBN 978-1-57344-214-5 $16.95

Spanked
Red Cheeked Erotica
Edited by Rachel Kramer Bussel

"Editrix extraordinaire Rachel Kramer Bussel has rounded up twenty brisk and stinging tales that reveal the many sides of spanking, from playful erotic accent to punishing payback for a long ago wrong."—Clean Sheets
ISBN 978-1-57344-319-7 $14.95

Rubber Sex
Edited by Rachel Kramer Bussel

Rachel Kramer Bussel showcases a world where skin gets slipped on tightly, then polished, stroked, and caressed—while the bodies inside heat up with lust.
ISBN 978-1-57344-313-5 $14.95

Best Erotica Series

"Gets racier every year."—*San Francisco Bay Guardian*

Best of Best Women's Erotica 2
Edited by Violet Blue
ISBN 978-1-57344-379-1 $15.95

Best Women's Erotica 2010
Edited by Violet Blue
ISBN 978-1-57344-373-9 $15.95

Best Women's Erotica 2009
Edited by Violet Blue
ISBN 978-1-57344-338-8 $15.95

Best Women's Erotica 2008
Edited by Violet Blue
ISBN 978-1-57344-299-2 $15.95

Best Bisexual Women's Erotica
Edited by Cara Bruce
ISBN 978-1-57344-320-3 $15.95

Best Fetish Erotica
Edited by Cara Bruce
ISBN 978-1-57344-355-5 $15.95

Best of Best Lesbian Erotica 2
Edited by Tristan Taormino
ISBN 978-1-57344-212-1 $17.95

Best Lesbian Erotica 2010
Edited by Kathleen Warnock. Selected and
introduced by BETTY.
ISBN 978-1-57344-375-3 $15.95

Best Gay Erotica 2010
Edited by Richard Labonté. Selected and
introduced by Blair Mastbaum.
ISBN 978-1-57344-374-6 $15.95

Best Gay Erotica 2009
Edited by Richard Labonté. Selected and
introduced by James Lear.
ISBN 978-1-57344-334-0 $15.95

Best Gay Erotica 2008
Edited by Richard Labonté. Selected and
introduced by Emanuel Xavier.
ISBN 978-1-57344-301-8 $14.95

In Sleeping Beauty's Bed
Erotic Fairy Tales
By Mitzi Szereto
ISBN 978-1-57344-367-8 $16.95

Can't Help the Way That I Feel
Sultry Stories of African American Love,
Lust and Fantasy
Edited by Lori Bryant-Woolridge
ISBN 978-1-57344-386-9 $14.95

Making the Hook-Up
Edgy Sex with Soul
Edited by Cole Riley
ISBN 1-57344-383-8 $14.95

★ Free book of equal or lesser value. Shipping and applicable sales tax extra.
Cleis Press • (800) 780-2279 • orders@cleispress.com
www.cleispress.com

Ordering is easy! Call us toll free or fax us to place your MC/VISA order.
You can also mail the order form below with payment to:
Cleis Press, 2246 Sixth St., Berkeley, CA 94710.

ORDER FORM

QTY	TITLE	PRICE
_____	_____	_____
_____	_____	_____
_____	_____	_____
_____	_____	_____
_____	_____	_____
_____	_____	_____
_____	_____	_____
_____	_____	_____

SUBTOTAL	_____
SHIPPING	_____
SALES TAX	_____
TOTAL	_____

Add $3.95 postage/handling for the first book ordered and $1.00 for each additional book. Outside North America, please contact us for shipping rates. California residents add 9.75% sales tax. Payment in U.S. dollars only.

* Free book of equal or lesser value. Shipping and applicable sales tax extra.

Cleis Press • Phone: (800) 780-2279 • Fax: 510-845-8001
orders@cleispress.com • www.cleispress.com
You'll find more great books on our website

Follow us on Twitter @cleispress • Friend/fan us on Facebook